HAIL OF DEATH

Coming around a boulder, Lane Jericho hunkered down when he spotted an Indian pony tethered farther to the east. He held there, his eyes squinting to unveil the position of the Indian.

"There he is," he whispered.

He levered a shell into the breech of his rifle, and this brought movement from the Indian, who rose up and hammered out two quick shots. This was answered by a slug from Jericho's rifle nicking the Indian's shoulder and making him drop out of sight.

"That ties it," said a disgusted Lane Jericho as Black Moon, snarling and chanting, began firing wildly with his rifle.

The gunfighter slid out his .44 Smith & Wesson. It would be close and bloody work now!

ERNEST HAYCOX
IS THE KING OF THE WEST!

Over twenty-five million copies of Ernest Haycox's rip-roaring western adventures have been sold worldwide! For the very finest in straight-shooting western excitement, look for the Pinnacle brand!

RIDERS WEST (123-1, $2.95)
by Ernest Haycox
Neel St. Cloud's army of professional gunslicks were fixing to turn Dan Bellew's peaceful town into an outlaw strip. With one blazing gun against a hundred, Bellew found himself fighting for his valley's life—and for his own!

MAN IN THE SADDLE (124-X, $2.95)
by Ernest Haycox
The combine drove Owen Merritt from his land, branding him a coward and a killer while forcing him into hiding. But they had made one drastic, fatal mistake: they had forgotten to kill him!

SADDLE AND RIDE (085-5, $2.95)
by Ernest Haycox
Clay Morgan had hated cattleman Ben Herendeen since boyhood. Now, with all of Morgan's friends either riding with Big Ben and his murderous vigilantes or running from them, Clay was fixing to put an end to the lifelong blood feud — one way or the other!

"MOVES STEADILY, RELENTLESSLY FORWARD WITH GRIM POWER."
— THE NEW YORK TIMES

DEATH RIDES THE ROCKIES

ROBERT KAMMEN

ZEBRA BOOKS
KENSINGTON PUBLISHING CORP.

ZEBRA BOOKS

are published by

Kensington Publishing Corp.
475 Park Avenue South
New York, NY 10016

Copyright © 1988 by Robert Kammen

First printing: November, 1988

Printed in the United States of America

CHAPTER ONE

One trembling hand hooked around the saddle horn when pain knifed through Lane Jericho's chest. There was this sense of great weariness, an unnatural fragility like hollow glass. The chilling message had come last winter, the pain along with a sick gray emptiness, to be confirmed as heart disease by a Southern doctor. You have a year, two at the most, came the grim prognosis. And Lane Jericho, wandering gunfighter, had accepted that. He left San Angelo the following day, setting a course toward the North Star, and maybe a hunk of land under it where his name and killing deeds weren't known. For along with the pain tearing at Jericho's heart was a desire to shed his guns. He wanted to die peaceably and in an unmarked grave, so that even the woman who'd left him would never know of his passing.

As the pain ebbed away, Jericho turned black-diamond eyes into the southerly wind and beyond the dimming horizon to what he'd left behind. The gunfighter was pursued more by the memory of those he'd killed than the law or others hankering to match their draw against his. Off to the southeast lay the

Black Hills and Deadwood, and a hardcase recently interred there compliments of Jericho's .44 Smith & Wesson. It hadn't been the case of Jericho sitting in a gambling casino holding aces and eights like Wild Bill Hickok. That hardcase had opened up at Jericho with a Winchester from an alley across the street, emerging from a drugstore, calling out the gunfighter's name, and levering shells that mostly shredded glass and splintered wood but did catch a piece of Jericho's shadow flung upstreet by the lowering sun.

"Another one," Jericho had mused bitterly at the time. He'd been here going on a month, idling around Deadwood and thinking of maybe homesteading south someplace in the Black Hills. The curse of his fame had clung to the gunfighter like a tick to a longhorn. He should have let his ash-streaked hair grow out like Hickok's, or grown a beard to complement a curling mustache shielding firm lips taut with anger. There was the sickening thud of a rifle slug punching into the horse he'd ducked behind, and quickly Jericho palmed his handgun and fired toward the alley while breaking across the street. He pounded onto the boardwalk as an errant slug cut through dusky light, and with the gunfighter's reflection gaping out of a wide and scroll-adorned window in Canberry's Dry Goods Store.

It showed Lane Jericho to be leaner than most his age—measured in calibers at .45. And though leaned out, he seemed deceptively larger than a man standing five-eleven in his stocking feet. Homespun black creaseless trousers were tucked into Justins, buffed and polished moments ago by a bootblack cowering behind his three-chaired stand in Mead's Drugstore. The shirt was a gray woolen fitting comfortably under the tan cowhide coat, but the Stetson was of recent origin; Tannenbaum's Imperial Clothing Store, one block removed from this sudden spate of violence. The craggy and somewhat hawkish face also mirrored in the windowpane had graced the pages of newspapers from Cairo, Illinois, to the Barbary Coast. Just recently there'd been still another picture of Jericho's trail-worn profile in the *Deadwood Sentinel*. The rather brief article had been just as unflattering. Notoriety such as this oftentimes led to inquiries from the local law, which had taken place a couple of days ago in the person of Sheriff Seth Bullock. The result was Jericho's firm promise to leave within the week.

Now, easing cautiously along the boardwalk under the curious eyes of those drawn by the gunfire, Lane Jericho wished he'd left this morning. He was hoping the ambusher would cut and run, that no blood would be shed. But the horse threshing about on its side told Jericho otherwise, as did two slugs gouging splinters near the corner of the building he lurked behind.

"Damned fools never learn," he muttered sorrowfully. Crouching down, he snaked his right eye around the wall to have it land upon a man with a rifle, whose hammer clicked upon an empty breech. And the gunfighter stepped into the dimmer light of the alley.

"Somebody'll have to pay for shooting up that drugstore," he called out to the ambusher, in the hopes the shadow-draped man wouldn't try for that holstered Dragoon. A vain hope as Jericho's Smith & Wesson bucked, twice more, the ambusher's drawn weapon falling just before he tumbled down.

Wearily, and with that killing fading into bitter memory, Lane Jericho brought his narrowed eyes up to still another flock of mallards veeing northward. *There* was freedom. Critters unrestrained by human emotions or laws. They'd reap what spring would bring, probably in that faraway tundra country. With the pain and that sudden spell of weakness ebbing away, Jericho tightened the rear cinch on his double rig and dropped the fender into place. By his estimate, that road a quarter mile northward and skirling to the west should be the stagecoach road from Bismarck to Miles City, Montana Territory. And, mounting the horse, he saw from this elevation the wide flood plain of the Yellowstone River. Once upon a recent time this had been pure Crow country; this gleaned from overnighting at the K-C spread. But this land being alien to him, Jericho, as he rode on, debated silently whether it would be better and safer to bypass Miles City. It had a reputation of being a big, blustery cow town, and with gambling and dance halls aplenty.

Grimacing at the sky starting to cloud up more, and a gust of wind fetching with it a hint that it would be a chilling night, the gunfighter brought his horse onto the rutted lane. Being used to sultry Texas weather, he finally decided that a warm bed and some brandy outweighed any risks he might encounter.

"Damned newspapers though," he remarked acidly, "have sure got me pegged as a badman."

Sighting chimney smoke, he tugged at his Stetson and spurred the horse into a lope, a wandering man seeking solitude with the desire to be left alone.

CHAPTER TWO

Recently a cowboy had pistol-whipped eight troopers of the 5th Cavalry and laid them out senseless in Maggie Burns's The 44, which claimed to be one of the fancier parlor houses in Miles City. Another item of note in the *Yellowstone Journal* was a row having taken place in Frank Reese's dance hall between soldiers from nearby Fort Keogh and local cowhands. A note of sadder proportions was the evacuation of Two Moons, Rain-in-the-Face, Spotted Tail, and other well-known Sioux chiefs to the Standing Rock Agency. Along with some promotional articles placed in print by the Northern Pacific Railroad, wholesale and retail dealers polluted the back pages of the *Yellowstone Journal* with sundry ads. And though Gilmer, Salsbury & Co., still had jerk lines hinging this cow town, for a modest price to the passenger, to Deadwood or Bismarck or Bozeman, many old-timers lamented that civilization was pressing down too hard upon Custer County.

From just being an outfitting point for hide hunters, and probably the most important market for buffalo hides in the Northwest, Miles City had become a major shipping point for livestock, the hub of considerable travel and commerce. The saloons and most gaming dens were open twenty-four hours a day, to accommodate both civilian and cavalryman. At night the doors of most saloons, weather permitting, were kept open. And so it was, a decade after Custer had ridden to glory over at the Little Big Horn, cowboys and trappers and locals paid no heed to a Crow passing along Main Street, with a squaw or two trailing behind guiding an Indian pony dragging a travois.

And the arrival of still another gunfighter in Miles City that evening went unnoticed. It was with little difficulty that Lane Jericho acquired a room at a boardinghouse. This was after he'd stabled his horse. On the way in, the bay had started limping, and after checking it out in the stable under the watchful eye of the hostler, both of them had agreed the horse had a condition known as sprung knee. He let the matter drop, reckoning in the morning to trade the horse for another.

After a scalding bath in a galvanized tub had removed the trail dust and a lot of weariness, Jericho put on some spare clothing. The clothes he'd worn he left with one of the maids to be cleaned. Since he was only a couple of blocks removed from Main Street, Jericho declined the offer of a cold supper and left the boardinghouse. The main thoroughfare, Jericho soon discovered, was narrower than in most frontier towns, and a heap longer, strung out toward the north and the Yellowstone River. And a heap louder too, judging from the noise blaring out of the saloons and gambling casinos. Stopping at the intersection to get his bearings, Jericho gazed first at the

11

imposing Inter Ocean Hotel, and in turn, Dewey's Golden Bar, The Arcade, and an eatery with the pretentious name of The Continental. This was where Jericho headed, and a little warily, as the street was crowded and lighted by street lamps. A lot of soldiers were in evidence, locals in suits and cowhands, an assortment of trappers, and railroad workers mingling among a few Indians and Chinese. But he failed to spot any hardcases, though it was a certainty others who lived by the gun were camped out here. Just before entering the restaurant, he passed a deputy sheriff, who cast Jericho a scrutinizing glance.

Much to the gunfighter's surprise the menu carried such entrées as loin of beef, Yorkshire pudding, strawberry tarts, and Edam cheese, all of which he ordered from a plump waitress fussing with a lock of light brown hair, and he commented to her, "Place is sure busy for a Friday night—"

"Mister, you ain't see nothin' yet. Come payday out at Fort Keogh it's pure bedlam in town." With a busy smile for Jericho, she bustled away.

Of interest to Jericho had been the new brick buildings strung along Main Street. From his experiences elsewhere, mostly in Western towns, he'd learned that fires were an efficient modernizer. The first buildings were generally of wood construction. Oftentimes there were haystacks within the town limits, a fire menace, another hazard being cigar butts dropped through the cracks in wooden sidewalks. Added to this was an inadequate water supply. The end result was that through sheer carelessness a lot of buildings went up in flames, as had been the case here, and in other towns in the Yellowstone valley—

Glendive, Billings, and Livingston.

Jericho discovered to his pleasure that the food placed at his table was tasty, which he washed down with several cups of chicory coffee and, afterward, a snifter of brandy. Then he lingered over a cigar while studying the happenings outside. Into his mind came thoughts of evenings such as this with Laurel, the dark-haired woman he'd married. She had been named after an evergreen tree from southern Europe by a father pining to return there. But to Lane Jericho she was the laurel wreath of victory he'd gained in marriage. Thinking back on it now, he couldn't believe they'd been together less than a year. That killing had done it, the one over at Waco, a duel forced on Jericho by a half-blood. After witnessing that gun duel, Laurel Jericho had told her husband to give up his guns and this gambling life or she'd leave him pronto. The next thing the gunfighter knew the woman he loved was gone, and this aboard a westbound stage. Pride had held him there, as it had kept him from searching for her all these lonely and drifting years. And he'd changed too, become honed to sudden violence and savoring the night life found in most towns like Miles City. Until finally, even before learning of his bad ticker, killing had become distasteful to him, and he even hated himself for what he'd become. But there was this damnable pride, the only thing that kept him going, steadied Jericho when these pensive moods came upon him, and a pride which just might bring about his undoing. Somehow, tonight in a town alien to him, Jericho felt that he might be gunned down here as well as anywhere else.

"You're gettin' morbid in your aging years."

"Another cup of coffee?"

"Nope, just sermonizin' to myself." Reaching to a chair for his Stetson, he rose, paid his bill, and left a larger tip than usual for the waitress.

Out on the street, he puffed on the cigar while debating whether to go and bunk down or try his hand at stud poker, one of his passions. As he stood there, Jericho's alert eyes ticked off the passers-by, a hard-earned instinct telling him if anyone professed more than a passing interest in a man standing out from others, by his carriage and .44 thonged down high at his right hip. A woman in a dress flaming so red that it seemed to throw off sparks drew a smile from Jericho as she hipped past him and linked up with three cavalrymen out for some sport. Like a black widow she veered them over to an open doorway and up a flight of stairs as Lane Jericho, the smile fading away, let a lumber wagon trundle past before stepping out into the street.

On the opposite boardwalk he sidestepped two trappers leaving a musky odor in passing, and slowed his pace. Then he pulled up short of a street lamp casting out yellow light. What Jericho saw was this: three men idling across the street, and with one other lurking in a narrow space between two buildings and bearing either a Greener or a long gun. The men lounged against the facade of a hardware store closed for the night, paying little heed to the activity on the street. All four men seemed to be giving a gambling casino, The White Lily, their undivided attention. Which was where Jericho had anticipated ruffling some cards.

"Only damned fools would try holding up the place," he commented tersely. "They ain't cowpokes either—more'n likely hardcases."

His interest waned, Jericho sauntered on and went into the casino. Easing away from the open doorway, he studied those at the faro layouts, his eyes and ears piercing through the pall of tobacco smoke, music, dim murmur of voices punctuated with a loud oath or two or someone calling one of the bar girls over. From a chuck-a-luck wheel, Jericho's attention took in the poker tables, and then a face registered in his mind before the name U.S. Marshal Con Tillison scrolled through it. He glanced at those crowding the bar, and back at Tillison again. The man had aged, as Jericho had done, but more gracefully; living on the proper side of the law, Jericho surmised, had some advantages. He eased to the front end of the bar, a crooked finger summoning a bardog, and thereafter a bottle of brandy and a shot glass.

The marshal seems to be winning, the gunfighter thought silently as he checked out if others had a similar interest in Con Tillison. Jericho's answer came in the form of still two more hardcases slouched at a back table. Seems, Marshal Tillison, you're boxed in, this judging from the eyes of the hardcases going constantly, and impatiently, to the poker table. He helped himself to another three fingers of brandy before slapping down two worn quarters, and then Jericho sauntered casually through the gaming tables. The chair to Marshal Con Tillison's left was unoccupied, and it scraped on the worn floorboards as Jericho pulled it away from the table and settled onto it. By rights, he mused bitterly, what happened to the U.S. marshal was no concern of his. They'd become acquainted down in Oklahoma, Tillison wanting to jail him for what proved to be a case of self-defense — Lane Jericho heading out anyway after a losing streak at poker. Afterward, Jericho had learned, U.S. Marshal Con Tillison had been reassigned to territorial Montana.

The rangy man was still unaware of Jericho's identity, since Tillison's eyes were on the cards he was dealing to the other five players.

"You seem to be winning . . ."

"Jericho?" was the softly spoken answer.

"Come here often?" he ventured just as softly.

The flare of surprise passing out of Tillison's eyes, he said, "Just riding through."

"Same's me, I reckon." Jericho fished out a small wad of greenbacks, then spoke more loudly. "I hope this isn't a closed game, gentlemen."

"Mister, you've a right to lose your money same's me."

"Obliged," said Jericho, and added softly to the marshal, "you got relatives living here?"

"You mean those two spearing me from that back table?"

"Those . . . and four more out front. What's the game, Tillison?"

"Surely not you, Jericho."

"That eases my mind considerable. Thanks for selling me some of your chips." Jericho picked up the five cards just dealt to him and anted along with the other players. He discarded three cards but kept the pair of nines.

"I heard you left Texas for good."

16

"By popular demand."

This provoked a tight smile from Con Tillison. "You won't like Miles City either, or Montana."

"You speaking professionally?"

"Just don't want you to unlimber that Smith and Wesson, Jericho. They say Oregon's right pretty this time of year."

Grinning, he said, "Marshal, you should have been a travel agent." His eyes slid to the three cards he'd been dealt, and quietly he folded his hand as Tillison dropped a couple of blue chips into the center pile.

"Still can't figure out, Jericho, this sudden interest in my current unpleasant situation?"

"Con, if I may call you that, why you're the only friend I've got here. Oklahoma's a long ways away. Besides, I respect a man for trying to do his sworn duty."

"You came that close from cloud dancing, Jericho."

"The fact is, Tillison, I'm here. And friends or not . . . or whatever side of the law we're on, it don't seem right and proper a bunch of scum going after one man, star packer or no." He dropped his hands to the armrests and shoved upward. Quietly he added, "I'm cutting out that side door and going out back to see if they've got some lurking there. Then I'll ease in the back door and try to get the drop on those two. That is, Tillison, unless you want to play this alone?"

Con stared back into Lane Jericho's black-diamond eyes, and finally he murmured, "Appreciate this."

"By the way, you got any deputy marshals along?"

"Not this trip."

"No matter; don't need deputizing anyways." Lane Jericho stepped around another table, found the side door, and let himself into a wide alleyway. From there he slipped along the wooden wall. Drawing the .44, he checked out the two outhouses and the shed, and beyond that, a slope-roofed building hovering over a corral. His eyes slid up to the branches of an oak tree slumbering off to the right, until finally he determined nobody was lurking out there. He tensed when the back door jarred open, then slipped behind a drunken carpetbagger reeling toward one of the outhouses and to the back door just closing.

In the back hallway, he debated over Marshal Tillison's presence here in Miles City. That a bunch of hardcases would want to take out a U.S. marshal in a town this size and unmindful of witnesses puzzled Jericho. That Con Tillison was alone also struck him as strange. Holding the gun down at his side, Jericho passed into a back room containing a few tables and a lonely billiard table to his left. He nodded at a couple occupying one of the tables, the woman, obviously one of pleasure, trying to entice a drunken soldier into leaving. The back room flowed into the main part of the casino divided only by support beams for the high ceiling. Closing on the table, one of the hardcases, sensing Jericho's presence, started to swivel his head, only to have the barrel of a gun jar against his nose.

"Had a gent down in El Paso move suddenlike and get his nose blown away. Seems this old .44's got a hair trigger. Any questions?" the gunfighter said softly.

18

"No . . . no," stammered the hardcase.

And to the other one Jericho intoned, "Just keep those hands cupped around that stein of beer . . . that's right. You boys are real cooperative, yup, real easy to get along with."

"Mister, you're making a mistake!"

"Why don't you tell all of this to Marshal Tillison."

"Nice work, Jericho," the U.S. marshal commented dryly as he came up to the table and studied the men seated there.

"We ain't done nothin' wrong, Tillison!"

"Probably not tonight. But, Grogan, your whole life has been one of crime and corruption."

"How'd you know my name, damn you?"

Curling a hand around the butt of his six-gun, the marshal eased it out before reversing his grip on it and clubbing the hardcase over the head; the man folded over his stein of beer. The other hardcase, anticipating like treatment, blurted out, "I'll not cause you no trouble, Marshal Tillison. I'm in this for the money . . . and that's all."

"In what?"

"Jericho, these men belong to a gang of gunrunners."

"Thought those days were about over, now that the Indians have had their run at killing—"

"It's a long story, I'm afraid. One involving our government and the Canadian. I'll take it from here, Jericho."

"There's some scum out front."

"I'll head out the back door with these two. Head them over to the Custer County jail."

"That's illegal, Marshal, since we ain't broke no

19

laws here!"

"Attempted murder for one, Tom Driscoll, then conspiracy against the United States Government, gunrunning, a heap more I can think of. I figure, with time off for good behavior, Driscoll, you should be breathing free air sometime in the twentieth century . . . that is, if your friends don't slash your throat first."

"Damn you, Tillison, that crap don't wash with me. Why, you can jail us here, me and Grogan, but come sun-up our lawyer'll be standing there with the bail money." Anxious eyes watched Marshal Tillison leather his six-gun and ease out a pair of handcuffs.

Holstering his Smith & Wesson, Jericho said, "Guess being a U.S. marshal isn't any picnic."

"Lately it hasn't been," agreed Tillison. "I owe you one, Jericho. But as I said earlier, try not to wear out your welcome up here."

"I'll tarry here just long enough to build up my stake at that poker table, Marshal Tillison. Just for the record, what do I tell those other hardcases if they come in looking for you?"

Returning Jericho's quick smile, the marshal said, "I just hope they don't connect you with me; could prove hazardous to your health."

· "For a fact I've never had any health insurance. See you around, Tillison."

Later, as Lane Jericho sat with five other men whiling away the evening playing stud poker, he was still pondering over that worried look he'd seen in Marshal Con Tillison's eyes. His guess was that Tillison was playing a lone hand in a very dangerous game. Gunrunning was nothing new, up here in Mon-

tana or down Texas way. And gunfighter Lane
Jericho had no intention of getting involved in the
law business, Tillison's or otherwise. It seemed ironic
that wherever he went trouble crowded right in.

"You in?"

"Yup."

"Didn't know you knew the marshal—"

Jericho gazed back at the seedy gambler riffling
the deck of cards across the table, and he said tautly,
"It's a small world. And getting smaller every minute."

The gambler, reading the impact of the gunfighter's words, said hastily, "My apologies if I offended
you, mister."

Nodding, Jericho swung his eyes to the batwings
brushed inward by a hardcase followed by another,
the men fanning out and looking for both Con Tillison and their comrades. Finding neither, they bolted
outside. Dragging on his cigar, Jericho surveyed his
cards, then bet heavily on the three kings he'd just
been dealt. The gambler folded, the other four men
tossing in chips and tired comments.

The night grew deeper, but it seemed just as
crowded in The White Lily as when Jericho had first
walked in, and he was winning. Once in a while he
felt a slight weakness of body as of a silky hand fluttering over his chest. Common sense dictated that he
fold soon and retire for the night. But he stayed at
the table, held there by winning hands and thoughts
of what had happened earlier. That he would see
Marshal Con Tillison again stabbed at his thoughts.
The feeling settled deeper in him that it was more
than mere coincidence his running into the U.S. mar-

shal. Irritated by the notion, Lane Jericho ordered a round of drinks for the table, tried to shake it away in a haze of blued tobacco smoke and the blur of cards fanning out from his hands as he dealt.

"Destiny," came Jericho's muted response, "has already dealt me a losing hand. So let that marshal fight his own battles."

CHAPTER THREE

A reluctant Lane Jericho left Miles City aboard a westbound Northern Pacific passenger train. He'd stayed an extra day, enjoying a winning streak at poker and a chance to rest from the rigors of being saddlebound. His ticket read Butte, Montana, another town unknown to him, but from all he'd read and heard about the copper capital of the world, Jericho knew it meant there'd be plenty of miners at the gaming table. And U.S. marshal or not, he meant to hang around a few days.

Around mid-afternoon he passed into the dining car and eased down at one of the tables. Ordering coffee and a sweet roll from a Negro waiter, he stared out at the passing landscape of prairieland fringing upon the flood plain of the Yellowstone to the north, browned grassland awaiting rain showers, while distantly ridged a few low buttes. A mellow sun raced ahead of the passenger train. Every so often Jericho spotted range cattle or small bunches of horses, and game animals, generally pronghorns, or coyotes skulking away from the monstrous black train.

Back at the depot in Miles City while waiting for the train to arrive, Jericho had been reasonably certain he'd spotted one of those hardcases, but in the rush to board the train with others he'd lost track of the man. As the memory of this returned, he glanced around at the other diners — a few cowpunchers, tradesmen, four miners seated at one table, and a sprinkling of sober-faced women seated with their families. The conductor, in passing through the car, nodded gravely at Jericho. Then his coffee was there, and the gunfighter lifted two cubes of sugar out of a bowl.

"Well, Mr. Jericho, may I join you?"

Glancing that way, he nodded at one of those he'd played poker with back at The White Lily, a seller of hardware named Adam Oberlander, and somewhat of a portly gent with a square ruddy face and an easy manner. "You can, Mr. Oberlander, but only if I buy the coffee."

"Since you have a considerable chunk of my hard-earned wages, sir, it's a deal." Settling down across from Jericho, he pulled out his handkerchief and began cleaning his bifocals. "And you are bound where?"

"Butte, for the moment."

"I'm debarking at Billings. Perhaps there I can retrieve some of my losses. A word of caution, Mr. Jericho. One of those men you helped Marshal Tillison arrest is aboard this train."

"I'll keep that in mind."

"And so is the marshal."

Frowning as he beckoned a waiter over, Jericho knew that if one of those hardcases had boarded the train, it was possible others would be aboard too, a fact which caused him to drop a couple of dollars upon the tablecloth and hasten to his feet. "Pardon my leaving, but I've an errand to run." Donning his hat, Jericho left the dining car and began working his way back through the passenger coaches. On his way up to the dining car he hadn't spotted Marshal Tillison, nor did he sight the man upon entering the last passenger car. Coupled behind this car were the sleepers, baggage cars, the caboose. Perhaps the hardware salesman had been wrong about that hardcase boarding the train. However, an uneasy gut feeling told Jericho otherwise. As for Con Tillison, he had to be holed up in one of the sleepers. Which meant that was where those hardcases, if indeed they were here, would be lurking in an attempt to kill Tillison whenever he emerged from his cabin.

"Why is it," grumbled Jericho as he passed through the vestibule, "that I have to wet-nurse the law? 'Cause all any lawman did was try to punch my lights out."

Hurriedly he went through the first sleeper car, and at its back end, drew up while keeping from being framed in the window in the closed door. It was then he glimpsed a lighted cigarillo held in a man's hand appear and arch upward and out of view again, and Jericho brushed the flap of his coat aside and slid out the .44. He inched ahead, to shortly hear the murmur of voices seep through the closed door along with the overriding clatter of steel wheels upon steel rails.

"I say we go in with our guns blazing."

"Relax, Grogan, that marshal will leave his cabin sooner or later."

"Tillison owes me, damn him, for hammering me

25

with that gun of his. Had no call to do that."

"Grogan, you're lucky he didn't ask you to go for that gun of yours."

"I can take him, anytime. Still wonder who that other dude was. For a fact he were no lawman." The hardcase Grogan glanced at the door opening, then his mouth gaped open at the sudden appearance of Lane Jericho. Maybe it was having his head laid open by Marshal Tillison's gun, or it could have been that the hardcase had built up such an edge to killing someone which caused him to wrench out his .45 Peacemaker. One slug from Jericho's Smith & Wesson slammed into Grogan's chest, driving the man back against the side door of the vestibule. The other hardcase froze, then watched helplessly as his gun was wrenched out of its holster, the butt of which glanced off his temple but with sufficient force to render him unconscious.

Still grasping the hardcase's gun in his left hand, Jericho shouldered into the last sleeper and dropped into a crouch as three more hardcases entered at its opposite end.

"Tillison!" he called out, hammering slugs at the confused men, one of whom dropped leadenly, and those still alive plunging back out of the sleeper car. "Tillison, you here?"

A cabin door was yanked open and the marshal called out, "That you, Jericho?"

"It sure as sin ain't the conductor," responded Jericho as he moved down to stare at Con Tillison emerging, armed, from his cabin. "I thought trouble always followed me around. Seems, Tillison, you're a regular disaster area."

"Obliged for this, but I thought you left yesterday."

"Pickings back at Miles City were too good."

"But glad you didn't. How many were there?"

"Two up front; three behind."

"Pretty even odds. Why don't you wait here while I finish the job?"

"And miss all the fun," smiled Jericho. He trailed after the marshal hurrying back to the vestibule, which was empty, while a check of the baggage car connected to it revealed to the two men that the door was locked. Prying open one of the vestibule doors, Tillison hung out to permit himself a backward view of the land to the east, and when he caught sight of three men trudging away from the railroad tracks, he came back in and closed the door and turned to Jericho.

"They'll have a long hike to the nearest town."

"Gunrunners you said back at Miles City?"

"That's right, Jericho, and operating up in that Blackfoot country. It troubles me how they knew I was coming up there."

"Meaning?"

"That only my immediate superior and the War Department knew I was being assigned to this."

"Tillison, this gets deeper all the time."

"Perhaps I've told you too much already."

"You haven't told me anything," came back Jericho.

"Well, you did save my skin."

"This happened over in China, I'd have to support you the rest of your natural life, Tillison."

"Come on, I've some liquor in my cabin."

"Before we tend to that, I gunned one of those

gunrunners down at the other end of this car. Knocked out the other one." The gunfighter went ahead of the marshal, only to find the conductor and others clustered near the vestibule.

"Marshal Tillison," the conductor said, "Did you kill this man?"

Jericho spoke up. "I had the honor of doing that. And it seems the other hardcase managed to get away."

"You must realize, Marshal Tillison, that I must report this to my division manager. The Northern Pacific has strict rules about gunfire aboard its trains."

"Report away, sir."

The conductor pulled out a note pad and looked at Jericho. "I'll need your name, of course."

"Hold up now," said Tillison. "First off, this is official government business. That dead man is a known criminal, gunned down by my deputy marshal, here, in the line of duty. Bill the U.S. marshal's office over at Billings for his funeral. Come on, Deputy."

In his cabin, Con Tillison closed the door and turned to Jericho easing onto a square-backed chair. Tillison said, "You ever hear of the métis?" From his valise he removed a bottle of Four Roses, then sat down on the bed and pulled out the cork.

"Seems that's a French word—"

"It's more than that. You ever hear of the Red River Uprising?"

"I can plumb tell you a heap of things about Old Mexico." He took the bottle from Tillison's outstretched hand and brought it to his mouth, and after a short drink, passed it back. "Métis? I do recollect

28

something happening up in Canada . . . some rebellion."

"This happened back in 1869, '70. Most of the rebels were half-breeds, or métis, those opposing the extension of British rule into a region that had long been almost independent." And as their train sped into the gathering darkness, Marshal Con Tillison narrated to the gunfighter Jericho the bloody story of an uprising led by one Louis Riel.

For decades the Hudson's Bay Company had ruled the Red River valley. It allowed the métis to live much as they pleased. Then in 1869, the company turned its rights in Rupert's Land, or Manitoba, over to the British government. The next year, Great Britain gave the district to the Canadian government, and plans were drawn up for developing the region.

At this time, the only people who lived in the great Canadian Northwest were Indians, a few traders, and about 12,000 Red River valley settlers. These settlers lived a simple life. They held no title to the lands they farmed. When they grew tired of a plot of ground, they moved on to some other spot which suited them. Suddenly road builders, surveyors, and officials descended upon the settlers. Their lands had been arranged on the old French plan of strips reaching back from the river fronts. Then the settlers became alarmed when these new officials told of a plan to rearrange the farms into townships and sections.

So it was that a leader rose among the métis. This was Louis Riel, a settler of French, Irish, and Indian blood. Upon learning that the Canadian government was sending out a new governor to organize the new government, Riel led the métis in an attack on Fort

Garry, now the city of Winnipeg. The métis captured the fort, and Riel set up a provisional government. Shortly afterward an assault by forces under McDougall was turned back. It was here that Louis Riel doomed the uprising when he condemned one of those he'd captured as a traitor and placed him, a young English Canadian named Thomas Scott, before a firing squad. The cold-blooded murder of Scott brought a large force of Canadian soldiers from the east, and as they approached Fort Garry, Riel fled into the United States.

"For some time now Louis Riel has been teaching at the mission of Saint Peter the Apostle. Mission's perched up near the Sun River."

"Why dredge up ancient history?"

"I'm afraid history is about to repeat itself." He declined the offer of a cigar. "Afterward, after the uprising fizzled out, a lot of métis headed west. They settled along the Saskatchewan River. Still nursing their hatred for the Canadian government. Matters weren't helped any by Louis Riel starting to teach at that mission. Riel's been sulking across the border, trying to set up another rebellion."

"Couldn't you use your authority as a marshal to arrest Riel?"

"Haven't any charges that'll stick. He's a cool one, Riel is. One thing that troubles me is that Riel was placed in an insane asylum over at Quebec. Could be they put him there just to get rid of the man." Rummaging around in a saddlebag, the marshal took out an oilskin map and spread it out on the narrow bed. "Compliments of the U.S. Army. The Rockies stretching north into Canada. Eastward, the prairieland of provincial Saskatchewan. Up there, and south along the Rockies, clear down to the Sun River, Blackfoot country. The Blackfeet respect no border lines—or us whites, for that matter. Those gunrunners have been selling arms to both the Blackfeet and the métis." He rose, placed a hand on a metal window brace, and stared out at the fleeing plains. "The fear of the Canadians is that the Blackfeet might unite with Riel's bunch of half-bloods. That being the case, Jericho, blood will be spilled all over Saskatchewan . . . and just maybe down here in Montana."

"Seems like a powder keg about to explode."

"Yup. And they sent me up to tamp the fuse." He nodded toward the map and gazed hard at the man sharing his bottle of whiskey. "The Blackfeet send their young 'uns over to that mission. Could be that Riel is teaching them more'n reading and writing."

"Seems this should be a job for the military."

"Washington doesn't want to create any international incident. They figure my getting killed up there can be hushed up. That happens, they'll probably send out another U.S. marshal."

"And I thought one in my profession had it bad." Grimacing, Lane Jericho stood up. "All of this jawing and that whiskey's made me hungry. I'll spring for dinner, that is, if you don't mind associating publicly with a known gunfighter."

"Jericho, I owe you more than a dinner." As Con Tillison folded the map and put it away, there appeared in his eyes a speculating gleam. "Couple of months ago I attended a meeting up at Helena—bunch of lawmen and military. One of them, the marshal of Arcadia, resembled you somewhat."

Jericho laughed. "If he was kin to me, he'd be wearing no badge."

Around an easy grin Marshal Tillison said, "Probably just coincidence that marshal looking like you. Or that his last name's Jericho — Brad Jericho . . ."

CHAPTER FOUR

The westbound train was long gone by the time Lane Jericho bought a horse to his liking and a Remington. His reasons for getting off here at Big Timber were muddied somewhat, and Jericho was still surprised at what he'd done. He was a man liking to think things through, since in his profession one learned to regret hasty decisions.

He set out around noon to the north, high loping the canelo along a trail pointed out to him by a buck-toothed clerk back at that general store in Big Timber. The cinnamon-colored bronc had fattened up from lazing in a corral and being grain-fed, and its rider was forced to rest it on occasion.

It wasn't so bad during the afternoon when Jericho could let the quiet and rugged bottomland along the stream he was following, the Crazy and Little Belt mountains sawing at the western sky, narrate to him the history here in Sweet Grass County, for with dusk came old memory chords picking and yammering at the gunfighter's thoughts.

His reasons for being here and not trainbound could be summed up in one word—Laurel. His wife, though of singular beauty, could be intolerably stubborn at times. And it was just possible she could have given him a son. Jericho was an uncommon name. Supposing the marshal of Arcadia, Brad Jericho, was his blood kin? Or even that Laurel was there? He could dismiss that marshal's bearing his surname as happenstance, but Con Tillison's description of Brad Jericho bore looking into.

Earlier he'd bypassed Melville, a small settlement of under a half-dozen buildings. Ahead lay still another upcropping in prairieland sere from the long winter. Tiredly the canelo found its crest to reveal beyond Harlowton glowing under an amber sky. Jericho, faced with the prospect of camping out or trekking another five or six miles, murmured, "Might's well head in for a hot meal and warm bed, hoss. Instead of me nighting out here in this fleabag. Gettin' cold, too."

Around nine o'clock he rode into Harlowton, a fairly large cow town, and the eastern terminus of the Montana Railway Company, a line strung across central Montana. More commonly it was nicknamed the "Jawbone Line," so named for its owner's, one Richard Harlow, fluent persuasion that substituted for cash in getting labor and materials. Harlowton, Jericho also learned that evening in a local saloon, lay where the Musselshell River fanned out into creeks.

"Heading north to Great Falls? Best bet's to cut through the Judith Gap; from there angle to the northwest. Could be tough going, since spring runoff has flooded the creeks and rivers."

"Obliged. Where's that dance music coming from?"

34

"Grange hall. Sort of a spring tradition around these parts." The grizzled rancher drained his stein of beer, and Jericho bought the cowman another before strolling outside. He gazed downstreet at the large building covered with galvanized siding that shone dully under moonlight, and around which buggies and horses were tethered. One of the covered surreys began to heave a little and its springs squeaked. Jericho smiled at the notion that some cowhand must have slipped into it with a local belle. Wistfully he turned and followed the glowing tip of his cigar back to his hotel.

Judith Gap, as Jericho found out, was really a town sitting in a gap between the Belt Mountains on the west and the Snowies eastward, the town having been named for the girlfriend of famous explorer Captain William Clark. He tarried only to water his horse, and at the edge of town, the sight of a smithy hammering a red-hot piece of iron into shape caused Jericho to rein over and tilt his hat back.

"Did a big, sandy-haired gent ride through recently?"

"Can't say as I noticed," the smithy muttered under cautious eyes.

"He'd be a U.S. marshal."

"He would, uh?" The man knew without asking that here was the genuine article, a gunfighter, which provoked a curious frown. "If this marshal came through, mister, it was before sun-up. Suppose you're hoping to catch up with your friends?"

"Friends?"

"Bunch of hardcases passed through couple of hours ago. Riding hard, too."

Lane Jericho headed out at a lope. The trail he followed along the passageway hemmed in by brush and cottonwoods and the mountains was deep-rutted, the result of bull teams hauling supplies down from the Missouri River port of Old Carroll to the mining camps in the Castle Mountains at Old Castle and Copperopolis. The canelo was less reluctant to keep up this pace, now that it had become accustomed to the trail. Another half-hour of hard riding brought up the sound of gunfire from the direction Jericho was heading. He said acridly, "Seems Con Tillison came this way after all."

Closer, he began to pick out the varying echoes of a Sharps and a couple of Henrys, the throatier roar of a Winchester. The terrain had heaped up some, the passage bouldery with a few pine trees, his eyes picking out tracks left by a stagecoach. Coming over a rise, he glanced at a flock of blackbirds fleeing upslope above the trees; pinpricks high in the dappled sky were turkey vultures. A horse whickering caused Jericho to draw up and swing to the ground. Tying the reins to a limber pine, he went on cautiously to settle among some large rocks. What revealed itself to the gunfighter was the stagecoach lying on its side, the shotgun and driver sprawled out beside it dead, and the four horses pulling it gone and probably halfway to the Missouri River by now. Sunlight glinted off the barrel of Con Tillison's rifle swinging out from behind the stagecoach, a slug from it chipping rock near a hardcase settled higher up.

Gradually Lane Jericho spotted the others raining

bullets down at the stagecoach—only four of them. That black hat with a red feather in its band, he recalled, belonged to one of those gunrunners he'd accosted aboard the westbound train. Nestling the stock of his Remington against his right cheek, Jericho sighted quickly and pulled the trigger, the gun bucking from the recoil of a slug that pierced daylight into the head of the gunrunner. He killed another, a shot in the upper chest, before the remaining pair realized what was going on and disappeared pronto. Only when Jericho heard their horses clattering away to the north did he climb down off the rocks and go back to his horse. Mounting, he rode on in. He came around the stagecoach and found Marshal Con Tillison sprawled limply against one of its wheels, barely conscious and blood staining his shirt and open coat.

Recognizing the gunfighter, he framed a weak grin. "This is a surprise."

"Dammit, Tillison," Jericho said crossly, swinging down and crouching by the marshal, "You knew they'd be trailing behind."

"Duty called."

"Duty'll get you killed too." He grimaced at the blood seeping out of the chest wound, and the paleness of face. "Slug's still in there, Tillison. And I'm no sawbones. Your only chance is my carting you back to Judith Gap."

"Probably won't last that long. So . . . so it *got* to you . . . Jericho . . ."

"About that marshal up to Arcadia carrying my name? Reckon you knew it would. You could have kept quiet about it."

"Figured I owed you. Re . . . remember you saying
. . . how it was over in China, a man saving another."

"You figure telling me could square things between
us."

"Figured right, maybe . . . I . . . I—"

"Easy, Tillison," said Jericho as he stood up and
turned to the canelo. From his saddlebag he removed
a spare shirt. "I'll try to bind and plug that wound
with this. Then catch one of those horses." Turning,
he stared in puzzlement at the badge Con Tillison
had palmed.

"I want you to take this . . . Jericho . . ."

"Touching it might poison my system—give me
consumption, or worse."

"As of . . . as of now I'm deputizing you."

"You're what? You're loco, Tillison!"

"I'm hit bad. Probably'll die before we get . . . to
Judith Gap anyway."

"Tarnation, Con, I'm the original sinner you read
about in the Good Book. I'd tarnish that thing a-
wearin' it. Besides, I know less about your side of the
law than any mortal living."

"Jericho . . . there's more . . ."

"I knew it," he moaned. He ripped the shirt down
its middle, and into smaller pieces. "No matter where
I go, no matter where on this green earth, there's always someone who knows me—or wants a piece of
my ornery hide."

"The marshal of Arcadia . . . could be . . . mixed
up with the gunrunners."

"For now, let's forget that marshal and your reasons for being here." He opened Tillison's shirt and
used his own to bandage the bullet wound. Then he

mounted up and went in search of the runaway horses or those belonging to the hardcases, and shortly he came upon two saddled horses hidden behind some boulders. Jericho brought them back to where he'd left Tillison. It was with some difficulty that he managed to hoist the marshal into the saddle, his efforts bringing a spasm of pain into Jericho's chest. Unsaddling the other horse, Jericho turned it loose before climbing aboard the canelo and clattering to the south.

Along the way U.S. Marshal Con Tillison kept rattling on between bouts of painful silence about the Blackfoot Nation uniting with those métis, and about other things of an outlaw nature going on up near the Sun River. As the settlement of Judith Gap appeared, Lane Jericho, in trying to piece together all that Tillison had said, came to this conclusion — that he should have stayed aboard that passenger train. But if he had, Tillison would probably be breathing his last up in the pass. Anyway, there was the marshal of Arcadia, and maybe Laurel, too.

CHAPTER FIVE

To the mission of Saint Peter the Apostle had come rebellious Louis Riel. Of mixed blood, French, Irish, and Indian, Riel was a slender man with a shock of unruly black hair and piercing almond-shaped eyes. The mission suited him, situated as it was around six miles north of the Missouri River and in an isolated section of territorial Montana. Riel appreciated the coming of spring more than the Black Robes for whom he worked as a schoolteacher, with Blackfeet children for his pupils. Soon there would be a cessation of classes here at the mission, but the fiery Louis Riel knew he would leave before then.

Troubling him at the moment as he prepared his noon meal in the log cabin assigned to him was the summons from Father Cataldo. The Jesuit was forever meddling in Riel's teaching methods, or checking upon him at odd hours. Could it be, Riel pondered, Father Cataldo had been contacted by the Canadian authorities? For Louis Riel must endure this dreary existence at the mission a little longer. He'd never killed a Black Robe, a man of the cloth, but Cataldo would perish if he even began to suspect that one of his teachers would, before this summer ended, lead another rebellion against the Canadian government.

The mission buildings and walls, constructed of stone, stood on a pleasant slope near Bird Tail Rock alongside the old Mullan Road. Last year, shortly before Louis Riel arrived, there also came the Ursulines, led by Mother Amadeus Dunne. Under Mother Dunne's guidance, thirty Indian girls were soon enrolled. The presence of these Blackfeet students also brought in a few tribal elders to check on what the Black Robes and their strange gods were doing to their children, for the mission fringed on the vast lands of the Blackfoot Nation. To the northwest lay Fort Shaw, while eastward the large trading town of Great Falls stretched along the Missouri. There were a few ranches in the area, notably the Powers Ranch and the Montana Cattle Company.

After Louis Riel filled a cup with herbal tea, he sipped from the cup while staring out a window to the north. This weekend he would ride up to the Blackfoot encampment where the Teton River came out of the foothills of the Rockies. The war chief, Red Cloud, would be there, and also a delegation of métis and the leader of the gunrunners. He could never bring himself to fully trust Jay Paragon, since he'd found out that Paragon had also been selling guns to the Blackfeet, along with giving them whiskey in exchange for favors from their squaws. The situation, as Riel assessed it, was getting out of hand. He could have his métis kill Paragon and the other gunrunners, but to do so would doom the rebellion.

"Dealing with scum such as Jay Paragon," he

mused bitterly, "is, after all, a small price to pay for taking over a province."

After Custer's 7th Cavalry had been massacred by the Sioux, the United States Army had placed more troops in their Western forts to crush Indian resistance. As a result, most of the Blackfeet had taken up permanent residence in southern Canada, in Saskatchewan and parts of eastern Alberta. The Blackfeet were a confederation of three large tribes, the Blackfoot, the Bloods, and the Piegans. They were a restless and aggressive people, handsome, superb hunters and warriors. Historically they had been constantly at war with the Cree, Assiniboine, Sioux, the Crow, even on occasion making swift and destructive raids against the Flatheads or the Kutenai, and also against tribes far south of their ancient lands in Montana. But their fiercest hatred had been for the whites, the settlers, ranchers, trappers, the pony soldiers.

Up in Saskatchewan, the métis, because of their mixed blood, had slowly gained acceptance among the Blackfeet. This grudging acceptance had given the métis many opportunities to visit the various tribes, and always they brought presents and talked seditiously against the Canadian government in the hope the whole Blackfoot Nation would join them in their rebellious cause. The Blackfeet, according to reports carried down to Riel by a few trusted métis, were getting restless, held in check only by Red Cloud. To complicate matters even more, Louis Riel had also learned that more Canadian soldiers were being stationed at outposts up along the Saskatchewan River.

Louis Riel was a passionate man of fiery temperament. He was prone to act in haste, as had been the case back at Fort Gerry when that young Canadian had faced a firing squad. Immediately public sentiment had cried out that the métis be disbanded, and Riel made to pay for this barbaric act. Ingloriously the leader of the métis had fled into the United States. And so it was, almost fifteen years later, a wiser and more embittered Louis Riel was determined that the mistakes of the past would not be repeated. If there were atrocities, they would be committed by the Blackfeet. This time they would be better armed and prepared, as already small bands of métis had stolen off to train with the weapons furnished by the gunrunners. And almost a month ago, at a meeting up at Saint Laurent, the métis had elected Riel president of a so-called provisional government. This, he realized, had by now been brought to the attention of the Canadian authorities. So, for Louis Riel, the die was cast.

Into Riel's troubled thoughts came this passage from Seneca, and with his deep-pitched voice murmuring, " 'Slavery enchains a few; more enchain themselves to slavery.' We shall be free . . . rid of Canadian interference—"

The sound of the bell tolling the hour of one brought Louis Riel out of his log cabin, where to his surprise he found Father Cataldo calling out to him.

"Ah, Riel, my dear Riel, may I walk with you?"

Riel simply did not care for the Jesuit, and he said bluntly, "If you wish. Word was brought that you wanted to see me—"

"How do you do it, Riel? I mean, how do you

43

make those Blackfeet boys you teach so—so obedient. The others who teach here insist they're mere savages. But you, Riel . . . truly I marvel at what you've accomplished in so short a time."

He gazed hard at Father Cataldo, trying to read what lay underneath those solemn brown eyes. Riel's eyes fled to a blackbird soaring over the stone wall and into the compound to flutter down near an oak tree. Finally, and still not trusting the unexpected compliment, he said, "It is merely a matter of discipline. I speak; they obey."

"It can't be all that—uncomplicated. Riel, I have been considering this, this intention of mine to have you, shall we say, train the other teachers—"

"In how to handle these . . . savages?"

"They are children of God. As we all are. Oh, what a glorious spring day."

"It'll rain tonight."

"Here, it is already one, and there isn't a cloud in sight."

"Tonight."

"Then it'll be a miracle, I'm afraid. Well, Riel, shall we set up some private consultations—between you and the other teachers—say, for this coming weekend?"

"This weekend will be an inopportune time, Father Cataldo. The Bloods insist I come up and visit their camp this weekend. I fear they want to see this mission teacher and judge whether he is still worthy of teaching their children."

"Yes, yes, Riel, we mustn't disappoint them. A splendid idea."

"It's a day's ride up to the Teton River. So don't

expect me back until Tuesday at the earliest." He nodded at the Jesuit and strode ahead of the man into a large stone building and sought his classroom

CHAPTER SIX

After resting up for a couple of days in Great Falls, Lane Jericho resumed his travels. He stood leaning on a railing of the ferry transporting him and the canelo across the flooded expanse of the Missouri. It was early morning, a trifle chilly, the warming sun just now inching above the buildings of the large town. The mood of the gunfighter was one of pensiveness. Yesterday, standing on a high cliff and gazing down at the falls for which this territorial town had been named, the sparkling mist rising from the falling waters, Jericho had considered tossing away the badge given to him by Con Tillison. Just toting it around, he mused grimly, could get him killed.

"Should never have promised Tillison I'd help him."

The ramblings of the wounded U.S. marshal on the way to Judith Gap had also included a reference to some major stationed up at Fort Shaw. It seemed strange to Lane Jericho that if the military couldn't stop these gunrunners, how could one lonely lawman get the chore done? Jericho could care less about gunrunning or métis. As a pronghorn will sometimes be attracted by a hunter flashing a red cloth or mirror, so it was that curiosity on Jericho's part was fetching him northwestward to a place called Arcadia and a man bearing his name. It could have just been deviousness on Con Tillison's part, mentioning that town marshal Brad Jericho could be hooked up with these gunrunners. Never trusted a badge toter—not for a minute.

"Much less want to impersonate one," he muttered sourly, and grimacing, he eased a cigar out of his shirt pocket and bit the end off.

"You say something?"

Jericho turned to the seedy man operating the crude log ferry, and after touching a flame to the cigar, he said, "What's up there?"

"Trouble.

"That so?"

"Injuns."

"Heard that."

"I still don't trust those Blackfeet. They've got a hate for us folks that's plumb unnatural."

"Whereabouts is Fort Shaw?"

"Sun River way. Heading there?"

"Maybe."

"Let's see . . . you're from Texas. Yup, no question about that. Lot of Texans relocated up there—cattlemen. Ever since, it's been just a running battle betweenst them Texans and Injuns over cattle."

"What about a town called Arcadia?"

"Freighted up there for a spell. That is, until them tarnable Injuns drove us off. Arcadia? Only town between Fort Shaw and the Rockies. A wild sort of place."

"How about its marshal—gent name of Jericho?"

47

"Jericho? Old Buck Windom is marshal."

"Appears he was."

"Doggonit, then Old Buck got hisself killed. In-juns must have done it. Then again, a lot of outlaws trailing through stop by for supplies. Like I said, Texas, a wild town."

"Being you're such a fountain of local lore, has there been any talk of some gunrunners operating up there?"

"Nope, not that I recall. You happen to be a law-man?"

"Gambler, among other things." He turned to his horse as the cumbersome ferry began nudging into the clayey bank. Then Jericho was in the saddle and loping up a cut in the bank to the snarling of a shaggy-haired mongrel darting out from behind a log cabin.

Two days after he'd caught his last glimpse of the Missouri River, with dusk settling fast around him, Lane Jericho hadn't come across any trails and saw only one cabin with its roof fallen in and surrounded by weeds and rusting debris. The front door hung open at an angle, and still buried in it was a broken arrow. Nearby flowed a creek through barren cotton-woods and lesser trees. He rode closer to the cabin and peered in a window, but somehow sleeping inside four walls where murder had probably been commit-ted by the Blackfeet didn't appeal to Jericho. So he rode over to the creek and swung down. Unsaddling the canelo, he let it drink before affixing hobbles to its front legs and turning it loose to graze.

Strangely enough, Jericho didn't feel tired from the hard riding he'd done. Could be, he mused, as he went about gathering firewood, leaving Texas and riding for long stretches at a time had shed some of that city fat, piled on by long years of gambling and just plain carousing. What had that sawbones told him, that the heart was a muscle that needed toning up from time to time. Bending to pick up another piece of wood, he held out his right hand.

"Don't flutter about as much," he muttered. A sort of lonesome grimace of a smile tugged at his lips, and then he set about making a campfire under a high bank shielding him from the northwesterly wind.

The canelo letting out a nervous whicker brought Jericho over to the horse, and quickly he cupped a hand around the horse's mouth. After a while he detected movement to the northeast, and Jericho leaned over and unstrapped a saddlebag and took out a field glass. Now he could make out three riders jogging southward. The one wearing a fur cap had long black hair spilling over his shoulders, and he was bearded. Another horseman wore a mackinaw, while all three men had the dark and swarthy complexions of Canucks.

"Could be métis," Jericho pondered. "Maybe on their way to rendezvous with those gunrunners." In any case, they didn't seem to be in any particular hurry. Cutting onto their backtrail with dusk settling fast upon the prairie could see Jericho losing them or riding into an ambush.

Waiting until the riders had passed into a long ravine, Lane Jericho got his campfire going. He

49

warmed some beans and store-bought biscuits in his old frying pan as flames ate at the blackened coffee-pot. It didn't take long to get cold at night up here, he'd found, a weather change that made hunkering close to the campfire a lonely event. Here he was, and Jericho had to chuckle at the thought, an aging gunfighter with a bum ticker about to get involved in law business. Let them métis, if truly those three riders had been that, go ahead with their rebellious work. He didn't owe Marshal Con Tillison a plugged nickel.

"The point is," Jericho chided himself as he poured steaming hot coffee into a tin cup, "I did owe Tillison for telling me about that lawman up at Arcadia." And what else had Con Tillison rambled on about after he'd been wounded, something about a major stationed over at Fort Shaw. Maybe this major and Tillison were working together on capturing those gunrunners. If so, the sensible thing for Jericho to do was head up to Fort Shaw, look up this major, and then give him the U.S. marshal's badge along with explaining what had happened to Con Tillison. Then he could ride out of there with a clear conscience.

But first light found Lane Jericho heading the opposite way and trying to pick up the trail left by the trio of riders he'd seen the night before. After a while he picked up fresh tracks venturing through wetlands sprinkled with small ponds. At Jericho's approach, a few mallards and some canvasbacks rose on beating wings over cottontails and red-winged blackbirds bobbing on reeds. Close at hand a meadowlark began singing as sunlight limmed the dusky horizon.

He urged the canelo across a creek to land sweeping upward into undulated prairie.

Out in the open in the uncertain light of dawning, with shards of mist still ghosting in low spots, instinct caused Jericho to urge his bronc up along a mesa wall and rein up among boulders that would shelter him from intruding eyes. Reaching back to a saddlebag, he took out his field glass. The trail left by those Canucks led southward, and Jericho wondered why they'd made no effort to hide it as he squinted through the glass at what appeared to be chimney smoke showing over a line of trees. Could be a town or ranch, he surmised. The morning chill had worked its way under his coat, and he snugged up the collar while thinking of the cigars reposing in a shirt pocket. His purpose in coming up here had been to spot their campfire.

"Wish Tillison hadn't told me about these gunrunners and all," he muttered. "Could be these Canucks are just down this-a-way lookin' for work."

On the verge of reining around, he paused when sunlight reflected off something on the prairie to the south, and he raised his glass. Then he located a pair of riders, and now a couple more, cantering out of a draw. He watched them closing in to pass alongside the base of the mesa. They were the same men he'd spotted last night. But the newcomer accompanying them was a genuine dandy in that solemn black suit and starched white shirt and string tie fluttering about as he rode cantering with the other Canucks. The darkish face under the flat-crowned hat kept turning to another horseman, and even at a distance of about a quarter of a mile Jericho could see anger glinting in Louis Riel's eyes.

According to Marshal Tillison, pondered Jericho, that mission where the leader of the métis, Riel, was employed as a teacher lay about in the general direction of that chimney smoke staining the lightening skyline.

In a little while the four riders passed out of sight, and Jericho came down the tapering wall to the eerie cry of a loon echoing to him from a parcel of wetland. He proceeded at a walk, northward, the cigar he'd just lit helping to warm him some. The sun was lifting itself above the landscape to reveal small patches of grass beginning that slow greening process. Spring, he knew would bring about the final snowmelt and make easy passage for those gunrunners up into Canada.

Once upon a time Lane Jericho had been a militiaman, a corporal with George Pickett's Virginia Division. They had come out victors in several battles against Union forces, giving false hope to the South that it would win the war. Then came Gettysburg, and that haunting and suicidal charge by the division against the middle of the Union Army massed atop Cemetery Ridge.

He could see it still, those shells bursting on top of the ridge and his fellow Confederates cheering as their ragged lines swept out of the woods and into the open. Now massive waves of return fire came from Union artillery, that mile-long line of which Corporate Jericho was a part wavering but charging on to the sustained screaming of the Rebel yell. Men went down, torn apart by bursting shrapnel, and also the few horses ridden by Southern officers. The fear came to him, a livid force so lethal it seemed to make his blood run cold despite the awful heat. This, he soon discovered, was only a prelude to the canister, millions of metal balls whirring at them like startled quail. Huge gaps appeared in the lines, which were lines no longer but men firing blindly, desperately up at the entrenched Yankees. The charge reeled, kept on at the shell-torn base of Cemetery Ridge, fell back to become a rout. It was then that Jericho felt that impact strike him in the back, but somehow he staggered on, wanting only to escape the death coming at them.

This was his memory of serving on the losing side, and afterward, the long ride to start a new life in Texas. Only there hadn't been many places for a Reb, so he'd hacked out a new life with his six-gun and a deck of cards. Then came Laurel, to stir within him the seeds of conscience over the profession he was in. Her leaving had been a bitter blow, more to his pride than anything else. Now he was tired of it all, a wandering gunfighter who didn't have sense enough to keep away from a place called Arcadia.

CHAPTER SEVEN

The dimming light lancing down from Scapegoat Mountain revealed the Blackfoot camp spread out between the western forks of the Teton River. Directly to the west lay a ridged shelf stained with tints of red and black; back of this the foothills embraced the tree-speckled lower slopes of the mountain. There was still plenty of snow at the crest of Scapegoat and other mountains chaining to form the northern Rockies, and Red Cloud, chief of the Blackfoot Nation, knew the plains would not suffer drought this summer.

The aging chief had ventured out of camp to this grove of budding aspens hacking out a defiant stand amid some pine trees. It was perfectly still, a sort of suspenseful silence that awaited a word from this solitary visitor to make the night sounds begin, perhaps a wind coming down that gap between the mountains or an owl cutting loose. There was a troubled set to Red Cloud's seamed face, and in his eyes that had viewed this land he loved for almost seventy years. His face was noble, with wide forehead, onyx eyes tinted with sadness, a firm mouth, Roman nose, and coppery skin marred with two old scars. He wore a simple buckskin suit and moccasins adorned with red beads, and since they were expecting visitors, he also had on an ermine horned headdress. Later, when Red Cloud returned to his lodge, he would exchange his upper garment for a war shirt trimmed with ermine tails.

Slowly, almost carefully, he turned and scanned the eastward plains becoming pocked with shadows and the mysteries of the night. There, for as long as Red Cloud could remember, flowed the buffalo river road—*Cokahlahishkit*. This broad road ran from the valleys east of the Rockies to the wide Missouri and Medicine River plains, where once buffalo had dotted the hills like stars in the sky. The Blackfeet would pounce upon vast herds of the humpbacked beasts and drive them over the mighty cliffs near Great Falls, where their squaws would hack away at the dying buffalo while shouting their joy at this good fortune, or sometimes use small arrows to kill the still struggling beasts and break the big bones with stone hammers to get at the suckling marrow, while the men gorged themselves on warm liver or fresh brains liberated from skulls by a blow from a hammer or on strips of intestine wrenched from the body cavities of the buffalo. Finally they would depart, their parfleches heavy at the ponies' sides, knowing at least for the coming winter there would be meat for all and that their medicine had been good.

At this moment, and more than ever, Red Cloud hungered for buffalo meat again. But it was not to be, for the great herds were gone forever. And out of this bittersweet sadness there passed from the old chief's lips a song of the Brave Dogs society.

"It is bad to live to be old. Better to die young. Fighting bravely. In battle."

And it was the members of the Brave Dogs society that Red Cloud feared most at the moment, since they were one of the more powerful warrior societies, with their leaders, chiefly Kills Two and the more sinister Running Elk, wanting to join these métis. Among the Raven Bearers and Kit-Fox, other warrior societies, there were many Blackfeet who'd voiced their decision to support Running Elk. Only two of the tribes, the Bloods and Blackfeet, had wintered in Canada, the Piegans living in small Indian villages north of the Teton River, and the Piegans, now that the buffalo had vanished, had turned to farming. Still, the younger Piegan braves treated disdainfully those who would plow open the land to plant seed.

But what all of them feared, and this included Red Cloud, was the increasing number of settlers coming into territorial Montana. And up in Canada it was no different. The limits of their ancestral lands were shrinking monthly, it seemed, something that inflamed a people unused to civilized ways. Somehow, Red Cloud sensed, he would be powerless to stop the inevitable, many in the three tribes of the Blackfoot Nation uniting in a war that made no sense.

Blacker grew the night, and Red Cloud's vision for his people. When the drums began beating, a steady tom-tomming from within the three ceremonial lodges placed together, he removed his hand from the aspen limb and began trudging downslope. As he appeared, a Blood, a member of the Black Soldiers society, those who were guarding the camp, stole past on his war pony, armed with lance, knife, rifle butt showing out of a doeskin case attached to his saddle. For a moment their eyes locked, respectfully, the Blood's entire body painted red, with wide black bands drawn across his forehead and chin. Two vertical black lines representing wolf's teeth were painted on his cheeks. His lance also was painted red, and attached to it at intervals were wolfskin strips. Draped across the Blood's shoulders was a wolfskin. He wore a legging and loincloth and a narrow headband of wolfskin having an upright tail feather fluttering over his braided hair. The reason this Blood, other members of his society, and other warrior societies were thusly adorned, was the expected arrival of Jay Paragon and his gunrunners. Also expected were other métis, some having already ridden in during the early stages of this week.

Tonight there would be celebrating, and perhaps killing, pondered Red Cloud, if those gunrunners tried to force themselves upon Blackfeet squaws. Some of the women, however, gave themselves willingly to these white men. But Red Cloud's greatest worry was that the gunrunners would bring in whiskey. Perhaps he should order his warriors to kill these white men, and drive out the métis. He stilled this impulse, for at the moment most of the other chiefs were keeping their thoughts and ears to Running Elk's oratory.

Red Cloud entered his tipi and told one of his three squaws hunkered down on the other side of the fire to light his pipe. For a time he sat there smoking, awaiting the coming of the gunrunners. He could hear the sounds of expectancy rippling throughout the great encampment, once in a while a war whoop, the drums, or a dog yip-yapping its displeasure. It was a life he enjoyed, one that had given him many wives and a fine herd of horses. One of the squaws came over bearing a bowl of food, a baleful glare from Red Cloud sending her away.

The flap stirred, and glancing that way, Red Cloud said, "So, it is you, Wolfskin Man. Come . . . come, share this pipe with me."

Reaching for a bearskin robe, Red Cloud pulled it over his bony shoulders and watched the leader of a society called the Braves hunker down to make himself comfortable.

Wolfskin Man took a puff and then spoke. "On the way down from Canada we discussed the unrest Running Elk is causing."

For a headdress the visitor wore a coyote skin, the tail hanging down his back. He wore a war shirt, fringed with weasel or hair locks, and leggings. The right half of Wolfskin Man's face was painted blue, the left red; black bands were around his wrists. He wasn't as old as Red Cloud, perhaps in his fifties, but there were strands of gray in his braided hair. He took the pipe from Red Cloud and inhaled deeply, letting the smoke pass from between his wide mouth before inhaling again. He did this slowly, ceremoniously, his manner one of deep respect for the chief of all the Blackfeet.

"Running Elk is but one man," Red Cloud responded.

"But one with great persuasive powers." A smile flickered in the warrior's almond-smoky eyes. "As much as he hates these white men, these gunrunners, I'm surprised he hasn't ordered his braves to kill them."

"Because they give Running Elk and these métis the means to wage war. We cannot win this war. They are too many"—Red Cloud waved a vague hand —"these pony soldiers. Word has been brought to me that more soldiers have come to Fort Shaw."

"These gunrunners have brought them."

"Yes, they have," Red Cloud said darkly. "If the pony soldiers attack our camp, we, of course, must fight back."

"Why would they do that? We are no threat to them. Unless—"

"Yes, Wolfskin Man, unless they know we have bought guns from the gunrunners. They could have learned this from the mounties of Canada. It is no secret to them that the métis visit us often. You remember, last summer, when Sergeant MacIver and some of his mounties visited our camp. We were told by Sergeant MacIver that we could live in peace so long as the Blackfoot Nation stayed clear of this."

"Helping Louis Riel and his métis?"

"But I am aging, my friend. No longer do the younger braves, chiefs, seek my counsel. They listen to men like Running Elk—Kills Two—"

"It is true."

"Can we truly say this land is ours anymore?" Red Cloud reached down and brushed a sparking ember back into the warming fire.

Wolfskin Man said bitterly, "How generous these white eyes are to call our ancestral lands a reservation. They want us to be farmers"—the Blackfoot grimaced—"like the Piegan."

"We will talk about this later," he said as several braves danced past the lodge, shaking rattles and beating drums, their defiant war whoops echoing back to squaws and children trailing behind. And after his guest had left, Red Cloud beckoned one of his squaws to bring over his ceremonial garb.

A sentry rode up as Red Cloud emerged from his lodge, and the horseman said, "The gunrunners are setting up camp east along the river." Wheeling his pony around, the sentry cantered away to inform the other chiefs.

In the moonless night the many lodges of the Blackfeet glowed like great candles with the light from their fires. In the air was a growing excitement, and everywhere in the encampment spread over several acres of grassland Blackfeet were moving toward the huge ceremonial lodge, the drumbeat coming from it growing louder. At the appearance of Red Cloud, other chiefs moved away from their lodges as did several leading warriors. Some of these chiefs wore the famous Blackfoot straight-up eagle feather headdress, with one of them, the leader of the Brave Dogs, having on a full coyote-skin robe. These headdresses were adorned with rows of brass tacks on the brow band and ermine pendants. A few chiefs wore a single eagle feather in their long black hair. Those assembling in the main lodge now were the men, the women and children to view the proceedings later.

The sentry on duty at the main entrance was a Blood, painted as were others guarding the camp. Entering, Red Cloud and the other chiefs took their places of honor.

Fastening another chief, Kills Two, with inscrutable eyes, Red Cloud said, "I see you have permitted your friends to be here."

"The métis are friends of all the Blackfeet," retorted Kills Two.

"Yes," cut in Running Elk, "it is known that our blood flows in their veins."

"This still does not make them blood brothers." Saying this, Red Cloud cast veiled eyes at several half-bloods clustered together at the opposite side of the vast encirclement of those seated in the lodge.

Now, to begin the ceremonies, the Raven Bearers flowed dancing into the lodge. Their chief carried a rawhide rattle and had a full ravenskin on his head; its wings were decorated with strips of porcupine quillwork, and a strip of red flannel hung from its beak like a tongue. He also wore a peculiar necklace made of imitation bear's claws carved from buffalo hooves or horn, along with a large gray wolfskin. Two other leaders of the Raven Bearers had on the same attire but carried staffs wrapped with black cloth and decorated with scalps, one staff painted red and adorned with eagle tail feathers like those of the dancing braves. The bearer of the black staff had painted his face red and then covered it with white dots to represent the raven's excrement. Except for their leader, every dancer also carried a feather-bedecked flag; quilled to it were raven feathers, that of the hawk, owl, eagle, and other birds of prey. They danced while facing inward, all the while imitating the croaking of ravens.

No sooner had the Raven Bearers finished their ceremonial dance and sat down in the vast circle than another warrior society entered the lodge, this being the Brave Dogs. They wore headdresses of bearskin with ears and two claws attached, war shirts of deerskin hung with rolled weasel tails, and large coyote skins, like ponchos, that nearly touched the ground. Their leader wore a horned headdress and led them in an intricate dance, while the singers carried sacred buffalo-hide shields.

Other warrior societies took their parts in the ceremonies. And only when the Kit-Fox society was performing did Jay Paragon, the leader of the gunrunners, shove past the sentry and come boldly into the lodge. Paragon, a tall dapper man with bold and ruddy features, smiled when the drummers stopped and all eyes swung his way. Sweeping the wide-crowned hat from his head, he bowed elegantly, and then addressed Red Cloud.

"Meeting you down here in Montana makes my trip a lot shorter." Then he settled the hat over his full head of longish black hair and strode arrogantly past the drummers and up to Red Cloud.

"At least you are here," said the elderly chief. "Did you encounter any pony soldiers on the way?"

"Don't worry, Chief, I know better than to lead them to your camp. This time I've got rifles aplenty."

"The métis want your guns. Not the Blackfoot."

"I say otherwise." The voice of Running Elk

dripped with sarcasm as his darting black eyes took in everyone at a glance. Quickly he stood up to strut before the other chiefs. "We are here, at our summer encampment. And for what purpose? To hunt the buffalo? No! And I grieve at this. We are here at the pleasure of the white men, who want us to become farmers. To raise crops in prairieland that rarely sees rain. We are warriors! We are not women! Here come our friends, the métis, to help us regain our lands . . . and our pride . . . our sacred honor. So what say you, Blackfeet, shall we become . . . women?"

The enraged and bitter shouts and war whoops of the Blackfeet beat at the hide walls of the lodge, and into Red Cloud's protesting ears. He came to his feet amid the uproar, and folding his arms, simply stood there enduring the verbal onslaught. After a long while, after the Blackfeet had quieted down, their chief spoke quietly.

"Much of what Running Elk said is true. The buffalo — they are gone. No longer can we hunt down in the Absarokas or spirit land of the Yellowstone. The Indian agents give us a few cattle to slaughter. They say we are no longer welcome nor can we visit the other reservations. They say we must stay on our lands here or up in Canada. They back up their words with the presence of many forts . . . many pony soldiers."

Spearing Running Elk with a stern glance, Red Cloud held up his arms as of one seeking wisdom from the medicine men scattered throughout the lodge or the Blackfoot god, what they often referred to as "a Spirit Who Rules the Universe."

"But must we sorrow as do the Cheyenne? Or Hunkpapa Sioux? The Shoshone? All of their great warriors, chiefs, perished when they warred with the pony soldiers. On the other hand, warriors of the Blackfoot Nation, we must not become lap dogs like the Crow. There are our children to think of . . . and our future—"

"What future?" blazed Kills Two. "Our future is in these guns brought to us by the white man, Paragon!"

Red Cloud held up a restraining hand, to say sternly, "Any decision we make must be without the presence of others. In two days all of the chiefs will assemble here. Is that agreed?" There were a few outbursts, but not from Running Elk, who sat there in stone-faced silence, and then Red Cloud leaned toward the gunrunner, and he whispered, "If you bring firewater into our camp, tonight or any other time, I will order my braves to take your scalp."

The dance continued well into the night without Red Cloud's presence, the chief having left to return to his lodge and worried solitude. Later, there was a feast of serviceberry soup and dog meat. And later still, Jay Paragon held a secret meeting in Running Elk's lodge, the leaders of the métis there, and Kills Two and some warriors.

Lurking outside the lodge around their own campfire were some of Running Elk's Bloods warily eying a half-dozen gunrunners. They were hardcases and drifters from the border states fringing onto Texas. Two of them, the Rayburn brothers, had escaped from a Louisiana chain gang; another, a wolf-faced

64

hardcase named Bo Layden, had broken out of the Oklahoma territorial prison. Foul odors reeked from their dirty ragtag clothing. But they were heavily armed, their weapons oiled and cleaned often, flushed with money, and just waiting for a chance to kill again. They'd murdered a few soldiers when breaking into those arsenals in Iowa and Kansas— gunned down some more when intercepting shipments of military hardware on information passed to them by a certain Regular Army major. At the moment they were passing around a bottle of corn liquor, the Western aqua vitae.

Inside the lodge, Pierre LaValle, the spokesman for the métis, gestured with his hands as he spoke in French-riddled English to Paragon, one of the other métis translating what was being said for the benefit of the Blackfeet. Because of the rising heat in the lodge, LaValle had opened his beaverskin coat, and a beaver cap was pressed over his shaggy black hair. He had an unkempt beard and blackish eyes.

LaValle said impatiently, "Paragon, we have discussed this before. The guns must be taken up into Saskatchewan. Now that the Blackfeet are down here, those soldiers from Fort Shaw will come more often. If they find any of those stolen weapons, there's sure to be trouble—"

"All I care about," the gunrunner said derisively, "is that I get my money."

"Heed my words or you'll receive nothing."

"Simmer down, LaValle," he replied around a tight smile. "I've got some howitzers this time—some Gatling guns, an awful lot of sidearms. Enough,

65

LaValle, for you métis to start a heap big ruckus."
Again that mocking smile flashed beneath the
trimmed mustache as Paragon hawked tobacco juice
into the fire.

Jay Paragon hailed from the City of Brotherly
Love, having left rather hurriedly during the last year
of the nation-dividing Civil War. He'd been a petty
thief and safecracker, but mostly Paragon had lived
off the earnings of a Philadelphia harlot. In him
there had been no patriotic stirrings when a captain
in charge of the military arsenal there sounded out
Paragon about becoming a gunrunner. That clandes-
tine partnership with Capt. Dirk Mackley netted Paragon a handsome profit, this from Confederate
agents in the form of Yankee greenbacks in exchange
for stolen arms. They would meet the Confederates
on an island westward in the Susquehanna River, and
it was here on a rainy summer night that one of Captain Mackley's sergeants turned out to be a colonel
from the Inspector General's office.

"That's right," said Sergeant Bristol as he stole into
the abandoned shack where Paragon and Captain
Mackley had been waiting for the Rebs to show up.
"Easy now while I relieve you gentlemen of your sidearms."

"What's the meaning of this, Sergeant?"

"To you, Captain Mackley, it's Colonel Bristol.
Selling arms to the Confederates is a hanging offense." Then his eyes darted to Jay Paragon, who was
spinning about to throw himself out of a window,
and he fired wildly.

As he picked himself up from the ground, Paragon

heard a couple of more shots followed by the gurgling sound of a man choking on his own blood. He drew his handgun, but held his fire when Captain Mackley stood framed in the doorway. "He's dead?"

"He is," Mackley said angrily. "I doubt if he found out too much of our operation since he'd been assigned to the ordnance depot less than a week. In a way I'm glad this happened, Paragon. The war'll be over soon, but it lasted just long enough for us to profit from it. Anyway, I've been told orders are being cut transferring me out West. This'll be our last arms shipment. What about your men?"

"They won't turn us in, if that's what you mean."

"Perhaps. But that's your problem. Just to be on the safe side, Mr. Paragon, I suggest you head out too. They say St. Louis is nice this time of year."

"Why don't I just kill you now, Captain Mackley."

"Because I've a hunch sometime in the future we'll have need for one another's singular skills again. I don't want to go through life living on a captain's pay."

And so it had been, after the Confederates had arrived to take charge of the packhorses, Jay Paragon, his saddlebags bulging with greenbacks, had swung his horse westward. He had gone to St. Louis, and from there to Old Mexico, had even spent a couple of turbulent years down in Argentina. Tiring of the sultry climate, a yearning to see the West again brought Jay Paragon aboard a clipper ship, the *Flying Cloud*. Disembarking at New Orleans, he secured passage on a train that carried him into Texas, and from there by stagecoach to Wichita. There, in a gambling casino, a chance conversation with a corporal brought the surprising news that a Major Dirk Mackley was stationed at nearby Fort Randall. The next evening Paragon found himself shaking hands with an older and somewhat heavier Dirk Mackley. And much to his surprise, he was told by Mackley about his being transferred to Fort Shaw, Montana Territory.

"Blackfoot country, Paragon."

"If you don't mind, I'll take Wichita. Once those red devils get a look at that hair of yours, Mackley, won't be long afore it'll be hanging in some brave's tepee."

"Hear me out, Paragon. Last year a month's leave of absence gave me an opportunity to get together with a half-blood named Riel. That was up at Great Falls. He heads up a band of renegades called the métis. Seems these half-bloods want to take over Saskatchewan. To do so, they'll need weapons. And if you, Paragon," the major went on, "will get some men together, we'll be back in the gunrunning business again."

The guttural voice of Running Elk tore that faraway gaze out of Jay Paragon's eyes, and the gunrunner stared into the Blackfoot's questioning eyes. Paragon said, "Sure, we brought some whiskey along. But you heard what Red Cloud said."

"We'll go to your camp, Paragon. There you'll give us whiskey. There we'll talk about the guns you have brought us."

Outside the lodge, as they began mounting their horses, Pierre LaValle grabbed Paragon's sleeve and muttered quietly, "There will be trouble if you give them whiskey."

"You see how many Injuns there are here. I figure what Running Elk wants, Running Elk gets."

"The guns . . . they must be taken into Canada . . . before any soldiers come here."

"Fork over the money, LaValle, and they're yours."

"Tomorrow. Louis Riel should be here tomorrow."

"Tonight, tomorrow, all the same to me, LaValle. Just how do you métis figure these Blackfeet will side with you?"

"For a long time we have cultivated their friendship. They are men of war, pure and simple, Paragon. A war that we shall win."

CHAPTER EIGHT

Established in 1867, Fort Shaw guarded the rich valley of the Sun or Medicine River, with its complement of 13th Infantry and 5th Cavalry policing the Blackfeet and other Indian tribes in their annual journeys over the passes to the west and down Sun River to the buffalo ranges west of Great Falls, over the famed "Great Medicine Road to the Buffalo." Chiefly, the fort was there to hold back the Blackfeet to the north and west and to protect travelers and goods on the dusty Fort Benton–Helena freight road, the principal commercial thoroughfare of the growing territory.

Blockhouses and log walls protected the soldiers and their families, the other civilians living there. An irrigation ditch from Sun River was used for lawns and trees and officers' gardens, making the fort an island of greenery and culture, what with its theater and dancing parties held in a special building. Fort Shaw's contact with civilization was a telegraph line built northward from Salt Lake City, and then to Virginia City, Helena, and on to the fort. Despite all of this, it was an outpost on the raw frontier dominated by the Blackfoot Nation.

Lane Jericho first glimpsed the fort when he rode onto the main road running to the west. Under a noonday sun he walked his horse in lingering dust left by a cavalry patrol that was just cantering through the main gates. The canelo had come up limping, and the first thing on Jericho's agenda was to have the horse reshod. Concern for his horse brought him reining up and out of the saddle. Then, the warming spring wind billowing around him, Jericho trudged toward the open main gates and a sentry slouching against the wall to keep out of the sun.

"You here on business?" the soldier called out as he shuffled into the sunlight, his eyes sliding carefully to Jericho's handgun. "Carrying your holster high like that means you've got short arms or you're a gunslick."

"I'm just a lost soul looking for a friendly face and a cooling drink of water." Shaping a curt smile, Jericho fingered out a cigar and tossed it at the leaned-out corporal.

"One of them imported cigars," the man said cynically.

"Who's commanding here?"

"A Frenchy name of De Trobriand; a colonel. Fought for the North during the Civil War. Now we're stuck with him."

"Then I'll be a-calling on Colonel De Trobriand," said Jericho. "That is, if I have your permission to proceed." And to himself, "Hope this redneck gets caught smoking that cigar while on duty."

"Proceed," responded the soldier as he plodded back into shadow and his own bitter reveries.

Lane Jericho passed through the gates and veered toward the stable area. The brick buildings, he noticed in passing, gave Fort Shaw a rooted permanent look, these sandwiched around older log and plank structures. A short row of brick houses — officers' quarters, he surmised — were picketed toward the Sun River, above which the vast compound was spread out on a grassy plateau. Back of the fort, to the south, lay a low row of hills and draws thick with brush. Several soldiers and some civilians were toiling away at the rising walls of a brick building, the brick actually being adobe, or big Mexican bricks, an idea borrowed from the houses of New Mexico. The bricks were made by a kind of masonry, half clay, half sand, with a binder of chopped-up hay. Closer to the river stood the brickyard where more soldiers were working. There were several blockhouses, and caisson and field artillery. Skirting the edge of the parade ground, he drew a few curious glances. The clanging of a hammer on an anvil brought Jericho between two stables and back of them to a smithy shaping a shoe. The smithy, sweating and bare-chested but with a red bandanna tied around his neck, glanced at the canelo limping up, and at the gunfighter.

"Nice hoss," he said pleasantly, and in a ricocheting Kansas drawl.

"Easy on a rider."

His eyes went to Jericho's deep tan, and he said, "Must be nice wintering down south. 'Cause these Montana winters can be cold and lonely. Reckon your hoss'll need shoes all the way around."

"Yup, I expect the others are just as worn."

"Expect I can get to your hoss sometime this afternoon. Just pay me for the shoes and a plug or two of tobacco." He nodded toward a corral.

"Thank you . . . sergeant."

The thickset soldier allowed a crooked grin to fan out his lips. "Was once or twice. You one of them connected with the Indian agency?"

"Just a drifting gambler."

"Last week of the month; you won't find much action among us troopers. The officers' club's another story though."

"That sutler's store back yonder cater to civilians?"

"There's a buck to be made, mister, Seth Watley'll smell it out."

Jericho lifted the saddle and blanket away from the sweat-stained back of the canelo and draped them on a corral pole. "You smoke?"

"Chew some."

Moving over, he passed to the smithy his remaining two cigars and said, "These importeds will chew just fine then. See you later, sergeant."

When he stepped out in front of the adjoining stables, nodding at a passing cavalryman as he did so, a few cold and scattered drops of rain tried to punch holes in the dusty carpeting of ground only to spatter up before fading away. The passing cloudbank was ribbed with bands of gray and an off-color white that all at once reminded him of that doctor's waiting room back in Texas. He still had breathless moments, but not as frequently as before. Just maybe, despite that doctor's grim prognosis, he'd be around to celebrate the half-century mark. This comforting notion was suddenly dampened by a downpouring of rain pouncing upon buildings, and Lane Jericho sought a doorway leading into the headquarters building.

Jericho found himself facing a cavalryman gazing up from his paperwork, the sleeves of his trim blue uniform festooned with wide yellow stripes from cuff to shoulder. Jericho said, "Sorry about barging in like this."

"This rain is what we need to settle the dust," replied Sergeant Major Gallagher. He was tall, sparse, the possessor of deep black eyes and thick black mustaches, and the top ranking enlisted man at Fort Shaw. "Could I help you with anything?"

A decision made by Jericho while trailbound was to play out the hand dealt him by Marshal Con Tillison. This was how he saw it, that Tillison's unexpected intrusion in his wandering life could gain him entry to places denied him before and just maybe a chance to shed his troubled past. What the tarnation, he was a gambler, among other things. Somehow the U.S. marshal's badge slid easily out of the fob pocket in his trousers to reflect a small shard of light. "Actually I'm here on official business. To see Colonel De Trobriand. My handle's Con—Con Tillison."

Dropping his pen on the morning report he was preparing, the sergeant major came erect while detailing his name. "U.S. marshals are a rare breed up this way. Mostly drifters come through, or ranchers, a lot of freighters. This is more or less Indian country, Blackfoot. You have anything besides that badge to prove yourself out?"

"As a matter of fact I have." He removed from a coat pocket an oilskin envelope, this produced from the personal effects of the man he was impersonating. Its contents, he told the sergeant major, were for the eyes of Colonel De Trobriand only, the official seal of the War Department backing up Jericho's bold statement.

"Regulations," the sergeant major said by way of apology. "Unfortunately, the colonel is busy at the moment." His eyes took in Jericho's dusty clothes dotted with drying rain spots. "You'll be needing quarters, a chance to clean up."

"A little soap and some hot water would ease these aching muscles."

"Corporal!" Gallagher called out, his strident baritone voice summoning a soldier from an adjoining room. "Take Marshal Tillison over to the officers' quarters and secure him a room. And don't dally getting back here. Marshal, the colonel will be free around four. I'll drop by and escort you to his office."

And with military punctualness Sergeant Major Gallagher arrived at four that afternoon to walk with Jericho back to the headquarters building. They passed still another construction site, and over the sound of hammers driving spikes into lumber, the sergeant major said, "We're one of two forts protecting the Fort Benton to Helena road. And until the Blackfeet are more or less tamed, Congress is determined that the civilians coming out here receive some protection. Which means more troops are on the way. This is more or less a waiting game. Meaning that until we receive orders from division headquarters we can't mount a spring offensive against the Indians."

"Just what trouble have they been causing?"

"This is the time the Blackfeet make their spring

migration out of Canada. They like nothing more than stealing horses, cattle, raising Hades in general. All the way down through Montana to the Yellowstone. Won't be too long before we'll be hearing from ranchers telling us about horse stealing and the like, and that some of their men have been killed. So far matters of this kind have been handled by the Indian agents stationed up in that Blackfoot country. The real problem is that settlers are moving in and claiming a lot of territory up there, and sooner or later there'll be a massacre or two."

"I don't envy you your job, Sergeant Gallagher."

"You get used to it," he replied, and slowed his pace when an officer called out to him.

"Sergeant, I've just received a wire that some replacements will be arriving in a couple of days. Along with another shipment of rifles. I trust we have adequate quarters for these men?"

"There's always tents, sir. But, yes, Major Mackley, one of the new barracks is ready."

"Sometimes your sarcasm wears a little thin, Gallagher." The major's disdainful eyes took in Jericho.

"Sir," said the sergeant, "this is Marshal Tillison."

Jericho nodded carefully. This could be the man the real Con Tillison had been rambling on about, but an inner caution kept him from revealing his reasons for being here. There appeared in Mackley's eyes a furtive gleam such as Jericho had often seen in the eyes of men on the dodge. The tight smile rippling apart the major's thick lips did little to dispel the notion in Lane Jericho that here was a dangerous man.

"Are you out here chasing some fugitive?"

"Something like that."

With a final glance for Jericho the major strode away, and as Sergeant Major Gallagher fell into step with Jericho, he said, "Mackley's a strange one. A loner."

"What does he do around here?"

"Quartermaster, along with being in charge of ordnance. And like the other officers, Major Mackley takes out a patrol from time to time."

"Something tells me you don't care for Major Mackley."

"It boils down to the way he treats his men." The sergeant major opened the door and followed Jericho into the headquarters building and down a barren corridor. A rap by the sergeant major on a door marked with the legend, Colonel Phillippe Regis de Trobriand, Commandant, elicited a command to enter.

The man rising from behind his desk to grasp Jericho's outstretched hand was tall, perhaps a couple of inches over six feet, and with a thickish build. The closely cropped hair was gray, the eyes filled with a cordial interest, and Colonel De Trobriand had a gray mustache and gray goatee parted to fan above his uniform blouse, which bore no epaulets but had brass buttons and fleur-de-lis parading across its wide front. He gestured toward a chair as Jericho passed the oilskin envelope to him.

"Marshal Tillison is it? Ah, that'll be all, Sergeant Gallagher. Oh, and Sergeant, will you inform my orderly I've decided to attend that dance after all?"

Settling down again, he used a pocketknife to slice open the envelope. Once in a while the sun poked out from behind scattering clouds and threw glinting light into the spacious room containing the large desk, some file cabinets, a few pictures and other mementos hanging on the walls and telling of De Trobriand's colorful past. There was one decorous picture, which Jericho glanced at, showing the colonel and other officers clustered around General U.S. Grant and President Lincoln at some army camp.

"You have the look of a man who enjoys a fine cigar." The colonel reached over to a small table and from a humidor lifted out a couple of cigars.

"That — and an occasional sip of fine brandy."

"That will have to wait until I'm off duty." He lighted Jericho's cigar first, then touched flame to his. "This affair tonight is more of a formal ball than a dance. We're expecting a few people from Arcadia, some ranchers and their wives. Functions such as this, Marshal Tillison, keep us from turning into savages."

"I suppose so, since Fort Shaw is off the beaten track."

"For that matter, so is Arcadia. I took over command here in February of this year. Managed to venture over to Arcadia; rather smallish. As for its inhabitants, a rather close-mouthed bunch."

"I understand outlaws drift in from time to time."

"So I've heard. But the army isn't in the business of pursuing outlaws and the like." Through the pall of cigar smoke, his eyes scanned the three-page letter. "Interesting. So you're here to go after some gunrunners?"

Jericho, shifting his weight on the hard-backed chair, related to the colonel his sighting those half-bloods from Canada, and that the four men when he'd last seen them had been angling to the northwest and into Blackfoot country.

"Yes, I know, those métis are stirring up trouble in Saskatchewan. As for Louis Riel, he seems to be behaving himself down at that mission school."

"Not according to the reports we've received on him, Colonel De Trobriand."

"That same statement was made by Sergeant Shawn MacIver of the Royal Canadian Mounted Police. MacIver has also expressed concern about these gunrunners. That they are selling arms to the Blackfeet. This letter, Marshal Tillison, also mentions that some of our arsenals have been raided."

"They are bold, these gunrunners. And dangerous. There is a possibility, sir, that someone in the military could be involved. How else would these gunrunners know when arms are to be shipped?"

With a thoughtful gesture the colonel placed his cigar on an ashtray. Then he leaned back in his padded chair and placed his elbows on the armrests while gazing steadily at his visitor. "You mean, if I read this right, that some of my men could be involved in this?"

"Perhaps," Jericho said carefully. "Enlisted men are poorly paid, as are some officers. What we are speaking of here, Colonel De Trobriand, is not hundreds but thousands of dollars. So the stakes are high, not only for the gunrunners, but for the métis. They will rebel—when, we don't know. We know they've been courting the Blackfeet."

"Which concerns me deeply, Marshal Tillison, since they're out of Canada now and encamped up along the Teton River."

"I would appreciate that what we discussed here stays between us, sir."

"There's Sergeant MacIver also. Rode out yesterday afternoon. Said he'd be back in a day or two. I suggest you two get together. Now, this letter says you're to have free rein in this matter. Since I command out here, I must insist you fill me in from time to time about what you've ferreted out."

"What if I can prove those under you are working with the gunrunners?"

"I hope you're wrong about this. In the short time I've been here, there hasn't been time to get to really know my officers and top-ranking enlisted men. And as you said before, the pay is barely adequate."

"Your ordnance officer, Major Mackley, what's your opinion of him?"

"Single, aloof, hard on his men. But a stickler for regulations. Why do you ask?"

"Just that the major would be aware of any arms shipments. Or receive any reports detailing theft of military arms."

"An accurate picture. Do you wish to see the major?"

"At the moment that won't be necessary."

"The way I see it, Marshal Tillison, you're about to head into dangerous country. Perhaps it would have been better if the Blackfeet had aligned themselves with the Sioux and gone against Custer at the Little Big Horn. That would have given the army an excuse to go against them. But they align themselves with no other Indian tribes. Do you seriously believe they'll join the cause of the métis?"

"The fact remains, sir, they are buying arms from

the gunrunners. And the Blackfeet are loyal only to their own kind. As half-bloods, the métis have their foot in the door. And their chief, Red Cloud, is getting old."

"Even if the Blackfeet do get involved in this rebellion, it'll be chiefly a Canadian problem."

"You give them enough guns and the Blackfeet'll take on the entire U.S. Army. Something that Louis Riel has taken into consideration. My only chance of heading this thing off, Colonel De Trobriand, is to find those gunrunners. That means heading for Arcadia."

CHAPTER NINE

Major Dirk Mackley was in a bitter mood when he pulled back into deepening shadows as the U.S. marshal and Colonel De Trobriand strolled past him along a plank walkway. There was a lot at stake here, a lot of money yet to be made, and it was the major's firm opinion that Marshal Tillison had been sent here to put an end to the gunrunning. About a month ago one of those working with Mackley had sent word that a meeting had been held southeasterly at Great Falls, and in attendance had been Tillison and the man who'd captured the Apache chief Geronimo, Medal of Honor winner Gen. Nelson A. Miles, along with some Canadian authorities. Under discussion had been the métis, of course, and perhaps the Blackfeet. It had been decided by General Miles that for the moment catching the gunrunners would be left up to Marshal Tillison and a Canadian mountie, Sergeant Shawn MacIver.

Turning away, Mackley passed down the side wall of the brick building and began crossing the parade ground toward his quarters, a pensive smile squinting his eyes. He had taken to drinking, the bulging waistline attesting to that, wanting to pull out of here before General Miles focused his investigation on Fort Shaw. A visit a week ago from Jay Paragon had held Mackley at the fort. The gunrunner needed at least two more shipments of arms, and after ten thousand dollars had been passed to Major Mackley, along with a promise of doubling that amount when the weapons were secured by Paragon's gunrunners, Mackley had reached out to his contacts in the military via telegram.

This was cold fact, something that Mackley could accept, even though he knew that a few soldiers might be killed when the gunrunners intercepted those arms shipments, one of which was leaving Denver a couple of weeks from now on a special train, another to be shipped out from Chicago.

But one thing Major Dirk Mackley could not accept was the refusal of a certain sergeant's wife to attend tonight's dance. On first setting eyes upon Hannah Colmar he'd lusted after the woman. She had russet hair spilling down her back and a sensual, full-bodied figure, and for the life of him Mackley couldn't understand her being married to a brute like Sgt. Flin Colmar. Hannah was the kind of woman who could quite easily grace the ballroom of London or Paris; out here at Fort Shaw she seemed kind of an enigma. There were other wives living this secluded life at the fort, the spouses of officers and enlisted men, but none so beauteous or bewitching as Hannah Colmar. Even the commandant, De Trobriand, had remarked on her singular appearance. So it was that Major Dirk Mackley must have her at any cost, even if that meant killing her sergeant husband. This last idea pleased him, took his mind, at least momentarily, from the arrival of that U.S. marshal. At the moment Hannah's husband was out on patrol, there being seventy-five men under the command of Captain Loman heading north to scout along the Teton River.

Now he thrust his full thoughts upon Marshall Tillison and the mountie. Obviously these men had discussed what they were going to do at that meeting down at Great Falls. Surely, as part of their investigation, they would check out the flow of arms into and out of Fort Shaw, but only if given permission, Mackley was reasonably certain, by Colonel De Trobriand. At the moment he couldn't afford to let this happen, since Mackley and those working for him here at the fort had stolen rifles, ammo, sidearms, and several Gatling guns, these weapons being taken by packhorse northwesterly and passed along to Jay Paragon and his gunrunners. So it came down to another sobering fact for Major Mackley, that he was living here on borrowed time. Which meant to him that Marshall Tillison and Sgt. Shawn MacIver, RCMP, must be killed.

And now that this cold-blooded decision had been made, Mackley swerved direction and sought the stable area. The horse he singled out was a bay, deep-chested and with a star adorning its forehead. Climbing into the saddle, he rode over and passed through the main gates and headed west along the main road. When the fort passed out of sight beneath the brow of a rise, he swung his horse riverward. Moonlight draped a golden band upon the swollen waters flowing to the east. He passed under cottonwoods and cedars and willows until he came to a draw in which there gleamed a small campfire. He brought the bay down the crumbly slope. Close to the fire stood an Indian cayuse whickering and pulling back from its reins that were tied to the broken branch of a fallen tree, while a hunk of venison hung on a spit over the low flames. Only when Dirk Mackley threw a leg over the saddle horn did he hear the ominous clicking of a rifle hammer.

"It's me, dammit!" Mackley called out.

Shortly thereafter a Sioux named Black Moon emerged from a copse of willows. Both men settled down warily near the campfire, and in broken English and Sioux the Sioux muttered, "There is no coffee."

"Doesn't matter," Mackley spat out. "What about Paragon, did he deliver those weapons to the métis?"

Unsheathing his hunting knife, Black Moon sliced away at the venison dripping fat into the flames. After a while he cast the major a short, curt nod. The Sioux trousers were of blue cloth with a red band decorated with copper buttons. He wore a buckskin coat, large copper earrings, the black, grease-slicked hair parted in the middle and hanging in braids secured by marten fur. Atop his head an eagle feather protruded from Black Moon's scalp lock. He was a renegade, one of those cast adrift by the Sioux. Presently he worked as a guide for Jay Paragon's gunrunners; next week could see Black Moon drifting into the Rockies again or southward on the plains to steal horses. He was loyal only to his dark passions. Black

Moon had killed three Crows and a Cheyenne, and a Rocking M cowhand.

These thoughts passed through Dirk Mackley's mind as he watched the Sioux cut a big hunk of venison away and begin gorging himself. "I asked you about those weapons. Were they—"

There was a fanglike curling of Black Moon's lips, a firmer grip taken on the hunting knife. At that moment the soldier was just another white eyes to be killed. As if gripped in the throes of a vision, he could see his knife slashing flesh to the bone. The fancy soldier's hat he would keep, perhaps the silken yellow scarf knotted around Mackley's thick neck, the Sharps and holstered gun.

"Two days ago Paragon reached the Teton River. The Blackfeet and those métis have the guns." A taunting smile revealed chipped and yellowed teeth. "On the way down here I spotted some of your pony soldiers."

"Just a routine patrol."

"I am to tell you that Paragon wants more guns."

Impatiently he replied, "Yes, yes. Tell him—tell Paragon that these things take time. Tell him that any day now a message will arrive at Fort Shaw telling me that another arms shipment is on the way. There's something else . . ." Removing a leather gauntlet, Mackley fingered three double eagles out of a tunic pocket, the disturbing and mournful wail of a loon fetching his eyes and those of Black Moon toward the river.

"My people say that someone will die when the loon sings. Otherwise, Mackley, why would you show

Black Moon your money—"

"A lawman showed up at the fort."

"And you want him killed."

"Will you do it?"

"What about the one from Canada, MacIver?"

"He headed out of Fort Shaw. Could be going back to Canada."

"Perhaps."

"You're not telling me all you know."

"The mountie, MacIver, rode to the northwest."

"Toward the Teton River?"

"The mountie MacIver is a great friend of Red Cloud. The great chief of the Blackfeet will listen to MacIver."

"It doesn't concern me the métis want the Blackfeet to side with them. But I don't like it, MacIver seeking out Red Cloud. How much more to kill that damned mountie?"

"You ask a lot of Black Moon. Before I began guiding for the gunrunners, I would have killed them just for the pleasure of it. Even you, had the opportunity presented itself."

"How much, damn you?"

"Twice what I'll be getting to do the job on that lawman."

Unnerved by the impassive eyes of Black Moon, the major from Fort Shaw tossed the money down and reached carefully for the reins of his horse, which was starting to drift away. He found the saddle, adjusted his grip on the reins as Black Moon called out.

"Paragon will meet you at Arcadia."

"Arcadia? When?"

"Two days from now."

"Damn him," Mackley blurted out as he spurred away into the sanctuary of underbrush and to a cut in the gully wall. This carried him up to prairieland, and sometime later, the stagecoach road.

"Damn Paragon anyway!" How could the man even suggest they get together at Arcadia. The isolated town was a known hangout for outlaws, any one of whom could know Jay Paragon, or the townspeople, for that matter. So far the finger of suspicion hadn't been pointed at Major Dirk Mackley. And then, too, soldiers from Fort Shaw oftentimes ventured to Arcadia to try the gaming machines or spend their meager salary on the few loose women. Thus far he had kept well away from the gunrunners by means of exchanging messages in a mailbox in the shape of a hollow tree halfway between the Sun and Teton rivers, an idea borrowed from owl hooters passing along the Outlaw Trail. More urgent messages had been brought to Mackley by Black Moon. Bitterly Mackley knew he had no choice in the matter, that he had to go to Arcadia.

With the ground lights of Fort Shaw revealing its stockaded presence to Major Mackley, he transferred his thoughts back to the immediate present—Hannah Colmar. She was a glittering jewel out here on the raw frontier, Mackley's need for the woman fetching his eyes past some ranchers he was following into the fort's vast compound and to houses occupied by noncoms and their families. Unless she had gone to the dance, Hannah Colmar would be there, and alone, since her sergeant husband was still out on patrol. In him she aroused primeval instincts, a deep and unsettling lust. Thus far he had kept his distance, nodding when they chanced to pass one another around the fort, Hannah's pace quickening as she hurried on, and always with Mackley trying to read the character of this sensual and aloof woman. Now, to the lilting sound of music seeping out of the ballroom, he rode directly to the stables and left his mount in the care of an enlisted man. Others were dismounting, ranchers, some cowhands, and from buggies and surreys those who'd come over from Arcadia.

"Evening, Major Mackley."

Checking his stride, Mackley half-turned and said pleasantly, "Mr. Yeager, nice to see you again." Vaguely he remembered that Joshua Yeager owned a store over at Arcadia and had something to do with the town council.

"I'm worried, sir."

"Still not satisfied that your new town marshal is doing a good job?"

"He's young, awful young. Been spending too much time out at the Bennett place sparking the man's daughter. Jericho's place is in town making sure law and order is maintained."

The situation, as Mackley saw it, was that the city fathers of Arcadia were more concerned about the profit they were making from the vast number of outlaws passing through. Arcadia was a town spawned by greed and blood, the sound of gunfire often announcing another killing over a game of cards or by someone just settling an old score. Every so often the army sent over a patrol, more of a symbolic gesture than anything else. On reflection, Dirk Mackley knew he was no better than Yeager or the other merchants, but where they were bound to a private hell called Arcadia, he could leave and never come back. However, here was an opportunity to explain his presence over there.

"In a couple of days I'll come over and hear you and the others out, Mr. Yeager. But from what soldiers who spent some time over there tell me, Brad Jericho is a more than adequate lawman. Perhaps he needs some more deputies?"

"Deputies cost money, Major Mackley," the merchant said curtly.

"We'll discuss it further over at Arcadia." Mackley swung around and headed for his quarters.

Passing his garrison hat to an orderly in the anteroom of the ballroom, Major Dirk Mackley eased around a group of ranchers only to be intercepted by another officer, Thomas, a captain with the 5th Cavalry.

Mackley said, "I understand you're being transferred?"

"Back to the Fourth Military District as aide to General Meade."

His eyes scanning through the wide arching doorway the ballroom, Mackley muttered bitterly, "How did you wrangle that choice assignment?"

"The general's son and I were classmates at the Point."

"Seems ability counts for nothing in this army." Arrogantly the major strode on into the ballroom and over to a corner bar. A glass of brandy in hand, he planted himself alongside an open window and stared out at the dancers spinning around to the music of a banjo player, a violinist, and an obese man plunking away at a bass fiddle. She wasn't one of the dancers, and Mackley's searching glance went to the crowded tables opposite. It was only when a seated woman bent down to pick up her fallen handkerchief that he caught sight of Hannah Colmar with her elbows hooked on the same table. Hannah wore a long, shimmering green dress, her russet hair up in curls held by green pins. She was smiling at a lieutenant who'd just drifted over to ask her to dance.

The band broke into a waltz, and after a second, Mackley placed his glass on the window sill and went boldly out onto the dance floor. The lieutenant protested only mildly as Mackley claimed his partner.

"I'm glad you came, Mrs. Colmar," Mackley said.

"Only at Colonel De Trobriand's insistence."

"Oh?"

"Something about sustaining culture, or orders to that effect."

"You puzzle me? The fact that a woman of your . . . obvious breeding is married to an enlisted man."

"The marriage suits me."

His arm drawing Hannah closer, Mackley said, "My apologies if I offended you. But you see, Sergeant Colmar has a rather rough way of dealing with his men."

"I've heard the same about you, sir," she replied

cuttingly.

He laughed into Hannah's eyes that showed a slight tinge of anger. He would have this proud-willed woman, despite the knowledge she held him in open contempt. For what Hannah Colmar didn't know—Mackley and a couple of enlisted men did—was that Sgt. Flin Colmar had been smuggling weapons out of Fort Shaw, and paid to do this by the man his wife was dancing with at the moment. Close-mouthed but with a quick temper, Sergeant Colmar was probably one of those men who didn't like others casting lusting eyes at their wives.

But for Dirk Mackley time was drawing short. First that mountie, now a U.S. marshal had arrived here. Perhaps within a few days a detachment from the Inspector General's office also. And there was Jay Paragon, coming to meet him two days hence at Arcadia, Paragon wanting more arms, and, too, a man, once this gunrunning operation was over, quite willing to blackmail him or inform military authorities for a tidy profit. As for ordering Black Moon to kill Marshall Tillison and MacIver, that was merely a delaying action. The others, Colmar and those two corporals attached to ordnance here at Fort Shaw would also have to be silenced. This the major would do himself—before the week was over.

"Enjoying yourself, Major, Mrs. Colmar?" a voice broke in.

Mackley flashed an engaging smile for the commandant of Fort Shaw dancing by with an officer's wife, his awareness more for the fragrant scent of Hannah's perfume. Gazing into her eyes, he again felt that terrible desire to carry her out of there and to his quarters. "I have," he said haltingly, "as we just discussed, a rough exterior. One does his best in this savage place. In peacetime we become the forgotten soldier. Perhaps in a year or two all of this will change."

"Yes, a lot of immigrants are coming out here. To take over the land of the Blackfoot, the Cheyenne."

"So far the rules of the game have been dictated by the native Americans. We—"

"The game, sir, will only be over when you've killed them all off."

Smiling, he said, "You sound like one of those . . . liberated women?"

"Only from the past," Hannah's eyes clouded over, and she pulled herself out of the major's arms when the dance ended and sought her table.

Within the hour Hannah Colmar left the ballroom. The night had cooled some, fetching up the swampy scent of the river, while off to the southwest lightning sliced out of an approaching summery storm. Drawing the shawl closer around her shoulders, Hannah set out across the parade ground toward the house she shared with Flin Colmar. Though the faint wind brushed lightly against her bare arms, still tingling her skin was the touch of Dirk Mackley, and she resented the bold way he'd held her, those mocking eyes. Suddenly there stirred in her thoughts a comment passed to her by Flin, of his being involved in some secret work with Major Mackley. Another thing puzzling Hannah had been Flin's coming into a windfall, the fact he'd been able to take her for a marvelous weekend down to Great Falls. There was a wealthy uncle of Flin's living back East, but between them had passed no letters. After living four years as Mrs. Colmar, she'd found her husband to be a roisterer, a man of dark moods, harder on himself than his men. She didn't love Flin Colmar, even though he'd rescued her from the wanton life she'd been living as a harlot in a San Antonio brothel.

Before that Hannah Colmar had waited, as had other wives, for her officer husband to come back from fighting the Apaches and Comancheros, the walls of Fort Brazos closing in day by day. So it was that one sultry day her husband had returned, draped lifeless over the saddle of his horse. Shortly thereafter she left for a San Antonio hotel, a woman aging into her thirties. In her had been a defiant frame of mind saying she would never return to Baltimore and that sheltered life, and a bitterness toward the military establishment. Then one day in the hotel's dining room, the charming Lucy Beaudine asked if she could sit at Hannah's table.

"I couldn't help noticing you."

"And why is that?" inquired Hannah over the rim of her cup.

"There have been no gentlemen callers. And you're far too beautiful for the likes of this place. May I continue?"

Hannah, after studying the older woman clad in an expensive black dress and veiled hat, said, "I've a feeling the Baptist church didn't send you over here."

Smiling as she spooned sugar into her cup, Lucy Beaudine said, "My discreet inquiries have revealed your officer husband was killed in the line of duty. And, Hannah, that your hotel bill hasn't been paid. I have a proposition that could prove mutually beneficial to both of us."

That evening Hannah found herself being introduced to the other girls working for Lucy Beaudine at her infamous brothel on the outskirts of San Antonio, and thus began a life that, after a while, threatened to destroy her. So it was that, some months later, Sergeant Flin Colmar chanced in to eventually fall in love with Hannah and finally take her out of Texas and to his new duty assignment here at Fort Shaw.

Upon entering the house she shared with Flin, Hannah turned on a lamp in the living room. As her shawl fluttered onto a chair, the sound of thunder coming through an open window, there was a moment of hesitation as Hannah deliberated over making some coffee. Instead, her eyes welling with a deep loneliness, she went into the bedroom and changed into her nightgown. Sleep came hard, the approaching rainstorm making its presence known, someone calling out to a barking dog from a nearby house, and with Hannah Colmar trying to sort out her troubled thoughts. That she would soon leave Flin was becoming more of a certainty. Army life out here, she had learned, was no different than that San Antonio brothel. And what she discovered only a couple of weeks ago was a cache of money hidden up in the ceiling by her husband. Four thousand dollars would help give her a new life down in St. Louis or Atlanta.

Sleepily she murmured, "Just how did Flin come

into that money?" Then her heavy lids closed and she fell into a troubled sleep.

The storm brought in sheets of much-needed rain water and served to clear the dusty air, but over the furious crackling of lightning came the scraping of wood against wood as an unlocked bedroom window was prized open. Hannah stirred on the bed, tried to open her eyes and find the source of this alien sound, only to have a large hand clamp over her mouth, the other arm of Major Dirk Mackley casting the thin coverlet aside. He tore at her nightgown, and though a terrified Hannah Colmar tried to get out from under his heavy, demanding body, the lusting Dirk Mackley showed no mercy to the woman he wanted.

CHAPTER TEN

Lane Jericho had been idling outside the ballroom when Hannah Colmar had appeared and slipped past him. She'd thrown him the briefest of glances. Jericho had been struck by the haunting quality of the woman's dark beauty, had had the wistful notion that it would be nice to shed a few years. And while relighting his cigar as he pondered over going inside, the corporal who'd shod his horse approached him.

"Gambler, been looking for you."

"That so? Care to go in and watch the festivities?"

"I had it in mind that we'd share a drink over at Seth Watley's place."

"Something tells me you've got more than corn liquor in mind."

Corporal Bagnelli, one of those fair-haired Italians with an engaging manner, smiled. "Some of the boys got themselves up a poker game."

"Army's changed some if'n they'll allow gambling at a military establishment."

"Out here there are few diversions. So for the sake of morale the colonel looks the other way."

97

"Long's things don't get out of hand."

"So far nobody's got hisself killed."

Falling into step with the corporal, Jericho said, "Won't mind taking some of that government money." Just before rounding the corner he caught a brief glimpse of Major Mackley stalking away from the lighted entryway and toward the parade ground.

The man ramrodding the game proceeding rather quietly in the back room of the store he owned had a hostile eye for the newcomers. Along with the big round table at which Seth Watley and four other men were clustered, merchandise was scattered about in untidy piles and on dusty, cobwebby shelves. Stacked there too were Mason jars filled with canned fruit. The musky stench of fur and mothballs filtered into Jericho's nose as Corporal Bagnelli called out the names of the players—Watley, Sergeants Weber and Calhoun, Doc Parsons, the post surgeon, and a lanky corporal with drooping eyelids, Martinsen. The newcomers elbowed places at the table as sutler Watley inquired as to their financial statuses.

"I'll start with a hundred dollars in chips."

"Fifty," ventured Corporal Bagnelli.

"Con Tillison?" Doc Parsons scratched at his rather ample beard. He'd removed his tunic, had rolled the sleeves of his white shirt to his elbows, and red suspenders came up over the sloping shoulders. Balding, he had a ridge of whitish skin along the upper fringes of his wide forehead and over the crown of his head. Behind the rounded glasses lurked crinkled eyes; and when the cigar wasn't clamped between his teeth, a constant smile tugged at his wide mouth. "Knew some Tillisons back East."

"Could be relatives."

"Well, Con, they call me Sweet Old Bob—or worse." Doc Parsons' cackling laugh brought one or two smiles.

The pair of sergeants, Jericho saw, were big, blocky men with the faces of those long used to the elements and maybe too many bouts with a bottle. The sutler resembled a tom turkey with that bobbing Adam's apple, big floppy ears, and longish and scowling face. He also had long tapering fingers that at the moment were riffling the deck of cards. Lastly, Jericho's eyes slid to the other corporal, Martinsen, and the considerable stack of chips the uniformed man had nestled between his long arms. Then, the cards sliding toward Jericho on the bare wood tabletop, he set his mind on the game, his cigar smoke trailing up and joining smoke already forming a thin cloud under the gas lantern hanging from a roof support.

It took Lane Jericho less than an hour to plumb the playing abilities of those at the table, and for one of the sergeants to curse as he dropped out of the game. Corporal Bagnelli left shortly thereafter, having gone through a run of bad luck. The other players settled deeper into their chairs, lit up fresh cigars, or helped themselves to whiskey provided by the sutler, for a price, of course. And which only served to point out to Jericho that Seth Watley had very few friends, if any.

Cupping his hands around the cards he'd just been dealt, Doc Parsons chewed a little harder on the stub of his cigar, followed that with a customary smile and spoke.

"I'll open with five silver dollars."

"You got something, Doc, or is this another bluff?"

"Ante and find out, Sergeant Weber."

"I'll call," came the sergeant's sullen reply.

"Five . . . and five more."

Under hooded lids Jericho studied Corporal Martinsen. The man had been playing with a sort of careless recklessness, winning some but losing oftener, and always able to fish out of his uniform pockets money to keep him in the game. Sometimes the corporal's eyes would lance out at Jericho in a hostile way, and he was drinking heavily, tossing down shot glasses of whiskey from a private bottle of corn liquor. Now, puffing on his cigar, Jericho studied the hand dealt him, a pair of deuces and three other low cards. Folding his cards and placing them facedown on the table, he curled his fingers around a stack of chips.

"Make that twenty," Jericho said.

"Awful steep," muttered the sutler, and with a sour grimace he discarded his cards.

Doc Parsons did a little beard scratching that was on the verge of being singed from the stub of cigar clenched between his teeth, and he scowled some before sighing wearily. "I'll call."

"Same here," Sergeant Weber said reluctantly as the sutler began dealing out cards to the other players.

Discarding three cards but keeping the pair of

deuces, Jericho filled out his hand of cards with three more but left them lying on the table while reaching to a nearby shelf for a whiskey bottle and pouring some of the amber liquid into his glass. He had been drinking sparingly, merely content to enjoy a friendly game of poker and not too concerned that one of the players would resort to violence as had often been the case down in Texas or elsewhere. But to him Corporal Martinsen was a puzzler, the sudden hunch of Jericho's telling him that the man was either a big winner at these weekly poker sessions or had something else going. The corporal had a rough, brazen manner, and sometimes spouted out sarcasm when he talked to Doc Parsons. At last, after sipping from his glass, Jericho picked up his cards — propped up in his hand were two more deuces.

"Ante's getting mighty steep," smiled Doc Parsons, "but I'll open with ten silver dollars."

"Make that fifty," the corporal chortled quickly, his chips raining onto those already piled in the center of the table.

"Damn," Sergeant Weber muttered as he threw in his cards and shoved his chair back and went grousing out the back door.

"Fifty you say?"

"Been watching you, Tillison," said Corporal Martinsen. "Played before, you have. But this time I've got you beat."

"I'll call that fifty — and a hundred more, son."

Groaning, Doc Parsons wavered as he studied his cards. "Watley, could you loan me some money, just until payday?"

"Nope," the sutler said flatly. "Against the rules."

"Dammit, Seth, can't you indulge an old man just this once?" He revealed his cards to the sutler. "Well?"

"Sure," the corporal said sarcastically, "it'll just mean more money for me."

"Watley, please?"

"Quit your whining, Doc, I'll do it . . . but just this once."

"Bless you, Seth, bless you." Doc Parsons laughed as he matched the bet just placed by Jericho, then to everyone's surprise he upped the ante another hundred. "I trust you, Seth, that you'll cover that too?"

"Got no choice, darn you, Doc."

"Last bet's mine. Call that . . . up it another hundred." Drunkenly the corporal let whiskey trickle down his shirt as he emptied his glass. "Well, gambler, you chickening out?"

"Son," Jericho said pleasantly, "your lack of respect for us older gents"—he nodded at Doc Parsons—"is uncalled for. And if your hand comes out of that side pocket with anything besides money, I'll blow some more hot air into your empty skull." Under the table the barrel of Jericho's handgun had just nudged into the corporal's whiskey-swollen belly. "So what's it to be, son?"

"Joshing was all." The words came out low and mean as Corporal Martinsen placed both hands on the table, and with Jericho knowing he'd just made another enemy.

Said Jericho, "I'll just call." He shoved some poker chips toward the pile, sensing that his four deuces would be bested, but adding quietly, "That's it, gents, four lonely deuces."

Corporal Martinsen's eyes sneered at Jericho, and he blurted out, "Not good enough, gambler. Four tens says I win." He slapped his cards down, faceup, and began reaching for the pile of chips.

"Hold it, sonny," cut in Doc Parsons. "Just feast your eyes upon a lovely straight flush! Now, there's some grand cards."

"That they be, Doc," agreed Jericho.

"Damn the lot of you," yelled the corporal as he shoved to his feet. He backhanded his remaining chips to send them flying against the wall shelves. "You ain't broke me yet . . . more where that came from. And I just don't like playing with crooks." As had one of the sergeants, the corporal exited, cursing and threatening to get even.

"I told you, Watley, I had the winning hand," smiled Doc Parsons. "Here's what I borrowed. And Con Tillison, it isn't every day four deuces gets beat out. Sorry about that."

"Playing with you has been a pleasure, Doc Parsons." Passing his remaining chips to the sutler, he received money in return, and though he had been one of the winners, it was just a little over a hundred dollars. As the sutler removed the chips and went about tidying the back room up, Jericho lingered at the table and passed the time in quiet conversation.

"Doesn't it seem strange to you, a corporal having that kind of money?"

"Martinsen's been in the game before. But come to think on it, Con, he rarely wins. This is puzzling."

"Probably something worth looking into."

"You struck me as we played as being something more than a gambler."

"Just between us, I'm a lawman."

"Interesting."

"Martinsen's lack of respect can be overlooked."

Laughing softly, Doc Parsons said, "These are rough men. But sooner or later those such as Corporal Martinsen will be taken to task."

"Still, I'd watch my backside."

"In a conversation with Colonel De Trobriand, oh, about a month ago, he mentioned there being gunrunners operating out here. Also, that he was fearful of weapons being stolen from our arsenal and passed along, to the Indians, I believe. Major Mackley was there too."

"Just between us, did Mackley assure the colonel that all weapons assigned to Fort Shaw could be accounted for?"

"He did."

"That's interesting."

Frowning, he said, "You believe otherwise?"

"Just don't know, Doc. I'm not about to accuse the major or anyone else at this juncture in time. Just the same though, it seems strange, a corporal having more money than an officer."

He followed Doc Parsons outside into downpouring rain. It was around two in the morning, and when they hurried past the ballroom on their way to their quarters, a few stragglers were coming out of the large building, ranchers and their wives who'd bunk down at the fort, and others. Clapping overhead went a long roll of muted thunder. Even now the rain was letting up, the clouds thinning out as they passed over Fort Shaw.

Stabbing a glance at his companion, Jericho inquired, "Generally officers don't play cards with the rank and file . . ."

"I'm batching it out here, Marshal Tillison. Got tired of doctoring back in Ohio after the missus passed away, some ten years now. Good woman, Millie. Wrangled myself a commission in the army on the condition I do my doctoring out here. Along with the pay, Tillison, I get three squares a day and a place to bunk down. How'd you like marshaling?"

"Lonesome."

Through a quiet chuckle Doc Parsons reached for the screen door and said, "You Texans sure have a way with words. I expect I'll see you at breakfast."

"G'night, Doc." Jericho passed the opposite way down the long corridor, and at its end, angled down another and shouldered into his room. He was just closing the door when the barrel of a handgun nudged into the nape of his neck.

"Easy, Marshal Tillison."

He found himself being guided, the gun still wedged into his neck, closer to the only table, where the man with the gun got the coal-oil lamp going before easing Jericho's gun out of its holster and stepping away.

"Turn around . . . slowly."

Lane Jericho knew it wasn't the corporal who'd just been in the poker game, and upon wheeling around on the two-inch heels of his Justins, he gazed back at a man a shade taller and darker of countenance. The hand gripping the .45 Colt was big-knuckled, steady, and he had on a plain buckskin coat coming down over his hips and black trousers that were tucked into gleaming black boots. The man's face was square, as was the mustache on his upper lip, the eyes were a steely blue, and the brogue, Jericho finally decided, more Irish than anything else.

"Mister, just who the hell are you?"

"You called me Marshal Tillison."

"It's late—and my patience is wearing thin."

"Colonel De Trobriand mentioned the Canadians had sent down a mountie. I'd say you're him."

"RCMP Sergeant Shawn MacIver."

"Well, then, Sergeant MacIver, we might as well make ourselves comfortable. How I chanced to bump into Con Tillison will take some time in telling. There's a bottle of whiskey in my saddlebags, some glasses in that cupboard."' Jericho removed his hat and tossed it on the bed.

"I've a hunch you're not a lawman."

"Nope. Gamble for a living. I'm Lane Jericho."

"There's a Jericho over at Arcadia—the town marshal."

"One of the reasons I'm up here, MacIver."

"No sense standing here," said Shawn MacIver as he handed Jericho's gun back and took off his cattleman's hat. "First, though, what about Marshal Tillison?"

"Got himself gut-shot shortly after leaving Miles City by some gunrunners. He more or less conned me into taking his place. That enough whiskey?"

Shawn MacIver nodded and found a chair at the table. He sipped at the whiskey, then said, "Not as smooth as we have up in Canada. So, Jericho, get on with it."

CHAPTER ELEVEN

On this Sunday morning the frontier town of Arcadia lay slumbering under a melony sun chasing shadows from the few false-fronted buildings tethered along Whitney Street, just a wide, dusty thoroughfare three blocks long. Creaking in the wind behind the buildings on the north side of the street was a windmill. Just west of that an old-timer named Boliver Payne was spreading handfuls of grain to a mixed assortment of chickens and geese outside his clapboard house. He had on bib overalls and a shapeless hat, a look at the clearing sky telling him it would get hot today. And stirring in the corrals by the two livery stables were horses wearing varying brands. Some of them belonged to a bunch of outlaws who'd strayed in during the week. Brushing a bothersome fly away from his whitish beard, Boliver Payne took a lazy glance at the street, and the smoke curling from the chimney of the Sunshine Cafe. Craving a hot cup of chicory coffee, he had it in mind to head over there or upstreet to Benson's Turkey Trot Tavern, its lunchroom also being open for business on Sunday. A rider coming from the south and moving onto the main street caught his eye, and the old-timer muttered.

"Marshal Jericho's up mighty early. Not much of a church goer. But he could have intentions of heading out to the Bennett place."

This morning Brad Jericho had taken special pains with his appearance, clad as he was in a new long-sleeved shirt and string tie bought earlier in the week at Goody's Mercantile Store, and he'd polished his boots and curried his bronc, a buckskin he called Lobo. The .44 Smith & Wesson lay high at his left hip, the marshal's badge winking back at the sun as Brad Jericho dismounted in front of the Turkey Trot Tavern. Except for his horse, the street was empty, the five other saloons closed now but generally opening their batwings within the hour. Out here, he'd learned, there was no respect for the Lord's day, nor any other, for that matter. He'd sort of lucked into the job, arriving here shortly after its marshal had been gunned down, Jericho's only qualifications being that he was handy with a gun. Coming onto his twenty-fourth birthday, sandy-haired and ruggedly handsome, he soon learned the town was a regular stopping place for men on the dodge, with the city fathers more than willing to trade with these passers-by as long as they had hard cash. Gunplay was almost a daily occurrence, petty thievery also, and there were plenty of bar girls to help entertain the outlaws and soldiers coming over from Fort Shaw. The job was getting to him, and if it hadn't been for Julia Bennett, he would have called it quits.

Ducking under the tie rail, Brad Jericho, from force of habit, gave the street a sweeping glance before pushing into the saloon. The Turkey Trot wasn't as fancy as the others, having no bar girls or roulette wheel. But the food served by Jingles Benson in his lunchroom drew a lot of locals. He strode through sawdust in the barroom and entered the lunchroom and eased down on a stool at the long and empty counter. Fingering a cube of sugar out of a bowl, he eyed Jingles Benson saying something to the cook, a Chinese named Li Sing, before passing behind the counter with a couple of cups of coffee.

"You're up early, Brad."

"Sundays are never quiet around here."

"New shirt?" Bailey set the cups down.

"Going out to Bennett's."

"Nice gal, Julia. Her pa, though, got some strange ideas."

Shrugging, Brad said, "Once upon a time John Bennett was a preacher. And to tell you the truth, Jingles, he isn't that much of a rancher."

"Takes time."

"Suppose so." He dropped another cube of sugar into his cup and stirred it around. Preying on Brad's mind, and what he didn't want to tell Jingles, was that John Bennett had been selling horses to some gunrunners. As a town marshal he

110

probably didn't have any jurisdiction outside of the town limits, and because of his love for Julia, he hadn't informed the military authorities over at Fort Shaw.

"Want the usual?" said the bar owner, and at Jericho's nod, he yelled back to the cook to rustle up some steak and eggs along with a side order of biscuits and gravy for himself. "How's Ray Green working out?"

"First time he's been a deputy. Likes being a lawman, which I'm finding out I don't. Today, if there's trouble—"

"Don't worry, I'll back him up."

On the slope of a foothill Brad Jericho stopped to let his horse breathe while gazing back at Arcadia some five miles to the east. He took off his Stetson and ran a hand through his thick sandy hair, more relaxed now that he was out of town and on the loose.

Looming over him were the high crags of the Rockies, dusted with snow, dominating the western skyline. Just being here made him feel at home, perhaps the same notion shared by mountain men who'd once roamed here freely. Out here there were very few ranches, since cattle were generally run more eastward on the open plains, and because of the Blackfeet. It still wasn't clear to him why John Bennett would want to start a horse ranch in this high country, though the valley his spread his located in had plenty of grass and water and soaring walls to keep the horses from roaming too far. A somber, tight-lipped man, John Bennett tolerated rather than liked him, Jericho sensed. As for Julia, why she'd picked him was still a mystery.

"There's others around better looking," Brad thought silently as he set his buckskin into motion.

The ride became steeper, with Brad loping along a faint trail running between rocky shelves narrowing into a canyon. With the shoulders of the buckskin laboring under him, he hunched forward in the saddle and came onto a level place beyond which, he knew, lay the wide opening to John Bennett's valley and his JB Ranch.

He was sweating a little, felt more limber from the ride and the cooling fingers of the wind knifing through the pass. He passed under aspens and Douglas firs, the track carrying Brad past windscoured boulders and to where the pass began opening onto the valley. In the distance and below in the lushy meadows he could see horses grazing, sometimes mule deer but no antelope as he'd seen out on the plains. Eager to see Laura again, he let the buckskin out a little on the downsloping track where the warming sun was bringing up the scent of pine. About halfway down the track he spotted a rider aboard a dappled roan coming his way along the trail leading toward the ranch buildings, and then Julia Bennett was calling out to him.

"Brad! Brad! I'm so glad you're here!"

They came together where the track flowed into the valley floor, two young people in love, and he said, "Didn't expect to see you up this-a-way."

"Pa sent me."

Now he could see her bulging saddlebags, noticed for the first time the worried set to her hazel eyes. Then she told him of some gunrunners arriving last night and of these men buying horses from her father.

"I can't figure your pa out. Sooner or later the soldiers will find out," he said.

"My father . . . he's different. Please, Brad, it's such a lovely day. I've . . . I've brought food along for a picnic. Let's ride over to Sapphire Creek and just enjoy ourselves." She leaned to him and brushed her hand against his cheekbone, the wind fanning out her blondish hair. She was small, around five-one, with big luminous hazel eyes revealing how she felt about Brad Jericho. Then, with his hand reaching for hers, Julia Bennett slipped out of the saddle and came into his arms.

After a while, he murmured huskily, "This valley . . . has so much going for it. For us, maybe. But I've a feeling, Julia, we're in harm's way. I figure my job as marshal is a day-to-day thing. Up here, your pa shouldn't be dealing with those gunrunners . . ."

"You know I just can't up and leave, Brad. We've talked about that before. Ma's dying changed everything."

"So you've told me," he said quietly. "I've saved up some money. Not a lot. Maybe enough to give us a start . . . someday . . ."

"Are you sure?"

"There'd be more, Julia. But I've been sending money over to Bozeman to my ma."

"Why, Brad Jericho," she said "you never told me that."

"Julia, there's a heap I never told you or anyone else."

"You're an honest man, Mr. Jericho. Come, let's head over to the creek. There's so much we have to talk about."

Shortly after the five gunrunners had ridden in at dusk last night, and after conferring with rancher John Bennett, they'd taken over the bunkhouse, forcing Bennett's three hired hands to sleep in the hip-roofed barn. Daylight found everyone out rounding up horses out grazing in meadows or secluded draws. The horses they found were driven back to the ranch and into big corrals, a task which consumed most of the day.

"Most of these horse have never felt the touch of a rope before," complained one of the gunrunners. "I'd say market price is too high."

"Driscoll, I was you, I'd button my lips," came back Bo Layden, swiping with the back of his hand at his sweating face. He had stringy black hair and a sallow face. Turning away from the cor-

114

ral filled with milling horses, he walked over to the rancher astride a gray horse. "Your horses are still a little peaked from having wintered up here, Mr. Bennett."

"They're good horses. Fifty horses. That comes to—"

"I know what it comes to," countered the gunrunner. "The only thing is, I don't have the money with me."

Displeasure took that watchful gleam out of John Bennett's deepset eyes. He gave the impression of being a bigger man than he actually was, dressed as he was in black clothing. Deep lines cut across his forehead, and alongside his thin mouth. He didn't fear these men, only what they could do to his daughter, and John Bennett saw no evil in dealing with these gunrunners. For once they'd departed with the horses he'd sold them, what happened then wasn't his responsibility. This unexpected bonus had allowed Bennett to pay off the mortgage on his ranch and salt a little away.

For most of his adult life John Bennett had been a Presbyterian minister. This had been down south, Louisiana, Georgia, a drifting kind of life where he stayed in one place for two or three years before moving on. There had never been any close friends. Before her death he had tolerated more than loved his wife. And he had sinned, against his wife and the church, taking up with different women at different congregations in his travels as a minister. This had led him to his last

115

parish, a large church in a Southern city, the passing of his wife there freeing him from the vows of marriage but binding him to the money he'd stolen from the church. Westward he'd gone, Kansas and Colorada and Wyoming, and finally up here to purchase a hunk of land he'd seen listed in a Billings newspaper. So his sins, he felt, were no greater than those of these gunrunners. But now that his daughter was on the verge of womanhood, John Bennett had been experiencing doubts about what he was doing.

"We'll be here a spell."

Angrily the rancher retorted, "I can't allow that."

"The others will be drifting in tomorrow or the next day. So will Paragon with your money, Mr. Bennett."

"I suppose it'll be all right."

"Supposing has nothin' to do with it," lashed out Bo Layden. "From here on in you just do as you're told. We'll be a-needin' some fresh beef."

"I have some cattle I'll sell you."

"Sell, nothing! Driscoll, take a couple of the boys and kill a couple of Mr. Bennett's steers."

"Got'cha, Bo. Maybe Mr. Bennett, here, will have that daughter of his fry us up some steaks. Maybe give us some lovin' later." Laughing at what was to come, Tom Driscoll and two other gunrunners ambled toward their saddled horses.

"I'm warning you, Layden, nobody touches my daughter!"

116

"Driscoll was just having some sport. This'll be the last time we'll be needing your horses . . . probably won't see none of us again. But I'll be a-warnin' you too, Mr. Bennett, play it cool and nothing'll happen."

"I'll say an amen to that," the rancher said coldly. Wheeling his horse around, he rode away at a walk.

He rode around the barn and out across a meadow and to a copse of aspens rustling in the slight breeze. Anger still filmed his eyes. These were very dangerous men, he was beginning to realize; and killers all. It was possible they wouldn't leave any witnesses behind, and though he didn't fear for himself, there was Julia.

"Sin," he said despairingly, "how bitter thy sting."

Remorse over his past, what he was doing now, flooded John Bennett's mind. Why had he forsaken the cloth? Dimly, in the reflected sunlight, he found himself, while gazing at the stirring aspens, recalling the biblical history of this tree. Recorded in the New Testament were the passages of how Judas Iscariot had hanged himself from an aspen, a circumstance which forever doomed it to tremble in retrospect. He was just as much a Judas himself, dooming his soul to hell, and perhaps signing Julia's death warrant when he struck that deal to sell horses to Jay Paragon. Here was truly a cold-hearted man, dealing out death and a smile at the same time.

117

"She must leave the valley!"

The rancher found his saddle and an eastward passage along the valley floor, a tract of virgin land some five miles wide and twenty in length. And later that afternoon, he came upon his daughter and the marshal of Arcadia in the process of saddling their horses.

"Pa," Julia called out, "is something wrong?"

"My daughter, you must heed my words." He swung down, threw Brad Jericho a quiet nod. "Have you told him about those men coming to the ranch?"

"She has," spoke up Brad. "That they're running guns."

"Well, then you know, Marshal Jericho. Which is why I want you to take Julia back to Arcadia."

"No, Pa, my place is here."

"I will brook no argument about this, Julia Bennett." Extracting his wallet from an inner coat pocket, the rancher thumbed out some greenbacks and pressed the money into Brad's hand. "Take her there—now."

"You figure these gunrunners will harm Julia and you, Mr. Bennett?"

"I have been told that this is the last time they'll come through to buy my horses. Those already at my ranch will be staying on until the others arrive."

"Then, why don't you come with us now?"

"There are my men, Marshal"—his hand swept out to take in the valley—"my home now. Julia,

118

you must know, though I've never told you, that I truly love you. You're all I have. Believe me when I say that my heart would break if anything happened to you."

Julia Bennett stepped up to her father and gazed with misting eyes at his softening face, and then her arms went around his neck, and she cried out, "I don't want to go. You know that, Pa. That I love you, too."

"If only I had loved your mother as much," he said gently. "Marshal, leave now, before they come looking for me. And take care, both of you."

CHAPTER TWELVE

"It was just our bad luck—Corporal Martinsen going out with that patrol this morning."

"The way it's been going lately," said Lane Jericho, recalling how those four deuces of his had been beaten out in that poker game.

It was now around mid-morning. Upon rising this morning both Shawn MacIver and Jericho had sought out the commandant of Fort Shaw. Where would an enlisted man get that kind of money, they'd asked Colonel De Trobriand, who in turn had looked at Sergent Major Gallagher's duty roster. From this it was revealed that Corporal Martinsen was assigned to ordnance and worked directly for Major Mackley as a clerk. After the colonel had promised to look into the matter, Jericho and Sergeant MacIver had left for Arcadia.

At the moment they were cantering along the stagecoach road some seven miles west of Fort Shaw and keeping an eye on thunderheads building to the southwest. While he was at the fort, Jericho had deliberated over having Doc Parsons check him over, but had decided against it since he was feeling better of late. And from the way his clothes hung on his leaning frame, the new notches in his belt, he could see him buying some clothes over at Arcadia. The thought pleased him, and he glanced at MacIver.

"It still puzzles me why Con Tillison wanted me to look up Major Mackley when I got to Fort Shaw."

"Mackley wasn't at that meeting at Great Falls," MacIver said.

"For a fact Tillison was talking out of his head after he'd gotten shot. Like you just said, the major wasn't at that meeting. Afterward, though, Tillison must have received word that Mackley was mixed up in this. Reason he was heading for Fort Shaw. Anyway, when I was introduced to Mackley as Marshal Tillison, the man was cool, real cool."

"He strikes me as being a rather cunning sort."

"Then you agree, Shawn, he's our link to those gunrunners?"

"Decidedly. Only we have to have proof. Going to Arcadia might give us that."

"By this you mean those who've been selling horses to the gunrunners. What about the marshal of Arcadia, figure he's involved in this?"

"Always a possibility." Sergeant MacIver nodded downtrail to where some blackbirds had just taken wing, and he pulled up.

"Saw some more scaring up before this," commented Jericho.

There was the dusty, rutted road, the hills and draws to either side, some buttes, northward the river breaks, gnawing at the sky in the distance the

Rockies. The wind was just a whisper barely stirring sedge grass and not strong enough to stir leaves. Clumps of trees, scrub brush, lay between them and the place where those blackbirds had flown away, and rocky ground.

"Could be a coyote or fox."

"Most likely it's trouble," Jericho said dryly.

MacIver's eyes smiled at his trail companion. "Your name's been hammering at me."

"Most likely thanks to it's being placed in the newspapers here and there. You'd tie it to me sooner or later. Down in the border states I'm known as a gunfighter."

"Well, Jericho me lad, we won't be holding that against you. If Con Tillison vouched for you, that's good enough for the RCMP."

"Mighty generous of you."

"Out here we mounties have to use every available source to keep law and order. And like it or not, Mr. Jericho, it became sort of official once you pinned that U.S. marshal's badge to your shirt."

"Never reckoned it that way, afore." They shared a quiet laugh, the tension going out of them, talking softly now as they outlined a plan of action in case more than a coyote had scared up those birds. "Another thing, MacIver, you're smoother'n buttermilk when it comes to palavering."

"I inherited that from my mother. Now, there was a woman." He reached down for his sheathed Winchester and trailed after Jericho as they left the road and angled to the northwest.

By Jericho's calculations, they had gone about a

half-mile, and a couple more blackbirds came in to land, then swooped away from a high rocky point guarding the road. Running up to this bluff were cottonwoods and elms, a creek cutting riverward at its base, and in the words of Jericho to the other horseman, an ideal spot for an ambush.

He whispered, "Shawn, I'll beeline toward the river. Try to pick up his tracks . . . come in behind him."

"One of those gunrunners?"

"Could be."

"Which only affirms my suspicions," said MacIver, "that these men have contacts at Fort Shaw. The stagecoach left shortly before we did; seems to have gotten through without any trouble. And some of those ranchers who came in for that dance used the road."

"Led a lonely life. So it's nice having someone keeping an eye out for you."

"You're a cool one, too, Jericho."

"Sometimes." He squinted toward the rocky bluff. "There seems to be some open spaces among those trees. Wait until you hear a meadowlark sing out, Shawn, then break out into the open."

"Just don't miss."

"Trust me."

"Guess I'll have to."

Jericho kept under shelter as he worked toward the river breaks. It didn't take him long to come upon a set of tracks left by an unshod horse passing to the south. After studying them, he realized they were dealing with an Indian, and worry began hammering at his mind. He'd encountered one or two in his wanderings, an Apache, a Comanche, managed to come out dead even, which meant he still wore his scalp lock. At a lope he went across an open spot and onto ground becoming rockier and sweeping upward. Swinging down, he left his horse tied to an elm branch, took out his rifle and crouched upslope. Large boulders shielded him from anyone lurking on the crest of the bluff, but also hindered Jericho from catching a view of the ambusher. Coming around still another boulder, he hunkered down when he spotted an Indian pony tethered further to the east, and scanned the land above him. He held there, his eyes squinting to unveil the position of the Indian.

"There he is."

Since he'd already levered a shell into the breech of his rifle, all he had to do now was alert MacIver, which came in the form of Jericho's lilting whistle—*tink-tink-a-link!* This brought movement from the Indian, who must have spotted the mountie, as part of his shoulder rose higher as he hammered out two quick shots. This was answered by a slug from Jericho's rifle, nicking the Indian's shoulder and making him drop out of sight.

"That ties it," said a disgusted Lane Jericho. "Just hope Shawn's all right." Quickly he broke away from the boulder and ran to the west and hugged in behind a pine tree. It would be close and bloody work now, which to the Indian probably meant a knife, the gunfighter his sidearm. He began blazing away at where he figured the Indian was concealed, broke away again, but upward this time to come out on the crest of the slope. They spotted one another at the same time, Black Moon snarling and chanting as he fired wildly with his rifle, and the gunfighter drawing but not missing, the slugs from his .44 Smith & Wesson punching holes in the beaded buckskin coat. Black Moon went down as Jericho closed in. He moved forward until he stood over the Sioux spewing out hatred from his black eyes willing a hand that no longer held enough strength to pick up the rifle.

"Can you talk?"

"Can . . . talk . . . but damn you . . . white man."

"Did someone from Fort Shaw tell you to do this?"

Black Moon coughed up blood and more hatred. "I tell you . . . nothing."

"No matter. Major Mackley told us everything after we arrested him."

There was a flash of recognition in Black Moon's eyes at that name, and he grunted out, "Mackley . . . all you damned whites . . . are cowards . . . despoilers of . . ." The spark of life went out of Black Moon's eyes, and he folded over.

"MacIver!" he shouted. "I got him!"

"And he got my horse! Of all the bloody luck!"

Jericho's search of the Indian's clothing produced the double eagles given to Black Moon by Major Mackley, and the saddlebags, nothing that Jericho could use as evidence. He brought the pony up to the top of the bluff, and after placing Black Moon over the saddle, returned to get his horse, then to make his way off the bluff and around it, where he found Sergeant Shawn MacIver seated on a mossy rock by the creek.

"Sorry about your horse."

"It was a good one. A . . . Sioux?"

"Yup, that he be. Found some money on him; around a hundred dollars. Though he didn't say it, he knew Major Mackley."

"Well, MacIver said as he rubbed his left shoulder, "A dying statement from an Indian would be thrown out of court anyway. So it was Mackley after all?

"I doubt if the man will confess if we bring this Indian in to the fort. Let's just play out the hand just dealt us."

"Meaning?"

"We'll bury the Sioux out here—turn his horse loose. Ride double the rest of the way to Arcadia. As for what happened to your horse, just that it stepped into a gopher hole and broke its leg."

"Then what, Jericho me lad?"

"Didn't Colonel De Trobriand mention that Major Mackley had set up a meeting over in Arcadia with the city council."

"Ah, lad, how truly devious you are. Are you certain you're not Irish?"

"Could be."

"It'll be just lovely to see Mackley's reaction when he sets eyes upon us. As for Mackley going there, Jericho, the place is a haven for outlaws. This is probably where he's been contacting those gunrunners. Their leader, we found out recently, is a rene-gade named Jay Paragon. And I'm sure that if we investigated Mackley's past, we'd find these men could have met before. Well, it's noon, or later. I don't suppose you brought a shovel along?"

"We've got knives."

MacIver sighed. "Yes, indeed we have."

A Swainson's hawk passed over them as they were scooping out a shallow grave in the barren ground under pine trees. After a while MacIver stopped to remove his coat. They were both sweating, with red-dish soil staining their clothing, by the time Black Moon was buried. MacIver uttered a few Christian words.

"A waste of words."

"Maybe it just took the edge off my anger."

"How much farther?"

MacIver used his bandanna to take another swipe at his forehead. "Between twenty and thirty miles. They always seem to know . . ."

Jericho grimaced at the circling vultures in the cloud-ribbed sky. "Just nature's way of keeping its house clean. Thirty miles is a far piece to be riding double. Be a lot more comfortable if you was to sling your saddle on that Injun cayuse. We can turn it loose just outside of town."

Casting Jericho a dubious eye, and with one for the pony, MacIver finally walked deeper into the trees. He returned carrying his saddle, bridle, sad-dlebags slung over a shoulder. Setting these items down, he pulled the rifle out of its sheath and leaned it against a tree. The pony started pulling away and rearing when MacIver removed the Indian saddle, which he dropped alongside the grave.

"Need some help?"

"Nothing I can't handle," came his testy response.

With a smile lurking in his eyes, Jericho eased down and leaned back against the trunk of a pine and tipped his hat back as the Indian pony began bucking in earnest when MacIver's saddle blanket was slid across its back. MacIver paused and stared at his companion taking a drink from a bottle of whiskey, and then MacIver set the blanket in place again, dropping the saddle on top of it, and somehow cinched it into place. He'd decided to use the halter already there so's to keep from getting a finger or two chomped off.

Stepping away and turning, he said, "You're sure enjoying this."

"You mounties ever drink on duty?"

He moved under the tree. "This seems to be an occasion that calls for it."

"Just don't kill the darn thing," said Jericho, taking in the mellowing late afternoon sun as it trekked lower over the Rockies. One massive thunderhead had jostled another aside to bully closer, but the northwest wind was shoving the cloud more to the east. And he mused: around about now down in Texas it would be siesta time, its drier heat being more to his liking. As for the mountie, he was a man who could be reasoned with, although to judge from the few scars and the one tattered cauliflower ear, Sergeant Shawn MacIver was no stranger to fisticuffs. About him, too, was a sense of purpose,

128

maybe a man to ride the trail with.

"I'll bet you've drunk on duty before."

Helping himself to another long swig of whiskey, MacIver smiled wickedly at Jericho. "Don't worry, I left a couple of fingers for you."

"Yeah, but I'll save the rest just in case I have to set a bone or two."

"You have a tender heart, Lane Jericho. You know, we can really upset Louis Riel's plans if we can stop those gunrunners."

"According to what Con Tillison told me, they're trailing up along the Rockies. He figured there's around twenty-five of them; that makes for a large operation. Like you said, Shawn, they'll be needing fresh horses again."

"I scouted out a few places west, southwest of Arcadia—horse ranches. But I didn't want to sound anybody out for fear someone might tip off the gunrunners. Once we do, though, our problems start."

"The two of us won't have much chance against that many guns. How about the law . . . over at Arcadia?"

"Helping us out? Maybe. As for the Blackfeet, Red Cloud as much as told me that he can see the handwriting on the wall for his people. They're a race that knows only one way of life—living off the land and nobody to tell them different. They're proud, aloof, distrustful of us whites, waging war is as natural to them as hunting buffalo."

"Only the buffalo are gone."

"But the Blackfeet as a nation is still intact. It's

129

the younger chiefs, Kills Two, Running Elk, who aren't willing to give up the ancient ways. And Red Cloud's old. I don't know . . . maybe heading this thing off'll take more than the pair of us."

"Colonel De Trobriand will send in troops if we find those gunrunners, or if the Blackfeet get involved."

"What we don't want is an Indian war." MacIver strode over and untied the reins, the pony jerking backward and rolling its wild cerulean eyes to show a lot of white.

"You know," Jericho called out, "maybe we should ride double at that."

"I can ride this cayuse," said MacIver through gritted teeth.

He tugged his hat down and led the horse out from under the trees and onto a meadow filled with rippling grass and prairie flowers. He brought the reins up around the pony's neck, hooked a firm hand on the saddle horn with his left boot working into the stirrup. The pony just stood there on stiff legs and cocking its head back at this strange-smelling creature, its nostrils flaring, and then when MacIver swung into the saddle, the pony sprang forward. The cayuse sunfished and squealed and bucked across the meadow, then broke into a frenzied gallop that brought it into thick trees reaching out for the man on its back and out of Jericho's range of vision.

"Some gents have all the fun," commented Jericho as he ambled over and mounted his horse. He brought it at a leisurely walk across the meadow, through the trees, and to where he could see the mountie still clinging to the saddled pony that was making westward tracks along the stagecoach road.

"Yup, sure beats riding double."

The stable Jericho rode up to still had lantern light pouring out to frame an open front door. Swinging down, he watched Sergeant MacIver trudging in, toting his saddle and possibles stowed in the saddlebags. Wearily the mountie moved past Jericho loosening the cinch as a yonker with a thatch of straw-colored hair poking out from under an old hat ventured outside.

"Sorry, gents, but I'm closing up."

"You'll be open a little longer," groused MacIver.

Having been here before, he knew Arcadia had some rooming houses and a hotel, the Frontier, frequented by men on the dodge. Other buildings of note were the jail, the only brick structure, the business places along Whitney Street separated by empty lots and a street having no boardwalk. Passing inside, MacIver checked out the brands on the stabled horses. He draped his saddle on a stall partition. As he claimed his rifle, Jericho led his horse into the stall.

Motioning the hostler over, the mountie said, "Son, do you have any horses for sale?"

"Reckon Mr. Peabody will know about that."

"You just work here part-time?"

"When I ain't helping out at my pa's place. We

got us a homestead up north about five miles."

"I'm not inquiring about your life history," said MacIver. "The owners of the horses stabled here, did they check in today?"

"Thereabouts . . . I mean, some came earlier in the week. Drifters, mostly; same's you."

"Is the town marshal on duty tonight?"

"Should be."

"Boy, you're a fountain of information."

Jericho stepped onto the center aisle and tossed the hostler a quarter. "You do a good job feeding and currying my horse and there'll be a dollar to go with that. You've been here before, Shawn, so where do we grab a bite to eat?"

"The Turkey Trot'll be open," the hostler said eagerly.

"That'll do," MacIver confirmed. "One more thing, son, that being I'll take it very unkindly if you mentioned that me and this other gent came into town together. Very unkindly, indeed."

"Maybe after you get done tending to my horse," broke in Jericho, "you'd best skedaddle for home. Make yourself scarce as rain water the next couple of days." He fished a silver dollar out of his pocket and shoved it into the hostler's shirt pocket. "Back a few years there was one such as you didn't heed the kind advice of my partner here. Sure wouldn't want to witness bloodletting like that again . . . no-sirree."

The hostler paled and gulped down his Adam's apple as his late-night visitors went out the front door. MacIver brought them onto a side street

132

lighted by a quarter moon shrugging over the eastern horizon. As he walked, he rubbed at his lower back, and murmured ruefully, "Wrenched my back when that damned Indian gunned down my horse. Just lucky I came out of that in one piece."

"Just lucky that Sioux was more used to chucking a spear. Where are we heading?"

"Mrs. Magstadt's boardinghouse to deposit our stuff. First thing tomorrow I'll call on the town marshal. I expect you'll be looking the town over tonight . . ."

"Just to get my bearings." Lane Jericho was glad the darkness shielded what he felt from the mountie. Ever since leaving Fort Shaw he'd been experiencing doubts about coming here, for rightfully, he felt, he should have never left that westbound train. He was too old to be scouting down a part of his past, and even if Brad Jericho was his son, he just couldn't walk up and say he was Brad's long-lost father. And more than ever Jericho felt his age.

Set behind a row of poplars, every third or fourth one dead and leafless, was a big painted house with a wide veranda. When they came through the trees, a woman seated in a rocking chair deposited her knitting on a nearby bench and pushed to her feet. This was Anna Magstadt, the offspring of one of Arcadia's founders, graying herself, the print dress clasped at her neck and encasing her large-boned frame. Wisps of gray hair stuck out through the hairnet, and when MacIver went up the veranda steps, she said, "You were here before. Want the same room."

133

"That'll do for me. Another one for my friend."

"Staying long?"

"Hard to tell right now."

"You know the going rate. Want meals, an extra six bits a day."

Upstairs in the privacy of his room, Lane Jericho peeled to his waist and scrubbed up at the washbasin. A towel in hand, he stepped to a window and gazed past the poplars at downtown Arcadia settled in for another night of gambling and drinking. This was a place that liked its law to tread softly. He'd known a lot of places like this, wouldn't return to any of them if he could help it. As for his passing as a lawman, the U.S. marshal's badge rested in his fob pocket, would remain there while Shawn MacIver poked about asking questions. Jericho would explain his presence here as that of a roving gambler. Donning a clean shirt, he strapped on his Smith & Wesson, pulled it out and spun the cylinder to check the loads. Leathering it again, he put on his coat and hat and left the boardinghouse.

Sauntering onto the main street, he kept to the shadows while studying the activity along it, horses tethered to tie rails in front of the saloons, or gambling casinos, while the respectable business places were closed for the night. He noticed some soldiers, the general run of locals passing along the street, and a few hardcases. He stepped into the street and headed toward a saloon where three older men sat before it on hard-backed chairs, none of whom so much as gave Jericho a glance as he shouldered through the batwings.

134

He thrust a boot on the bar rail while watching the barkeep sell a new deck of cards to a mule skinner. Lining the bar were some cowhands, with four merchants hogging the front end of the bar, and at its back, a soldier leaning on his elbows while nursing his drink. Up on the wall behind the bar a big framed sign advertised Coney Island Club sour mash whiskey; other signs detailed brands more familiar to a wandering man like Jericho. A lamp salesman must have passed through, since the lamps hanging in tethered clusters in the high-ceilinged room were more decorative than was usual for a frontier town. On the potbellied stove there was a container used to heat water, and the saloon had the usual number of poker tables, only one of them seeing any action. A quiet word to the barkeep produced a handful of cigars and corn liquor poured into a shot glass.

"Any big games going on?"

"All we've got here is nickel ante poker. There's plenty of gambling places here, mister, like McFaddan's or the Green Edge casino."

"I do thank you." He spun a double-eagle piece on the bartop, which the barkeep palmed as Jericho studied those standing to either side. That first glass of whiskey went down smooth and easy. As he poured another from the bottle left by the barkeep, the cowhands decided to leave, and Jericho found himself eying the soldier setting down his empty shot glass.

"Seems like you've come onto hard times."

"Hard times is being in the U.S. Army."

"Had my share of it, soldiering. Here, shove that glass over."

Affixed to the man's sleeve was a lonely yellow stripe, and the private appeared to be in his twenties. He was ruddy of face, the uniform blouse unbuttoned and needing to be pressed. "I do genuinely appreciate this, mister."

"I take it you're stationed at Fort Shaw."

"Going on a year now." The private came over and stood next to Jericho. "You're new around here?"

"Passing through." His eyes flicked to the barkeep spilling his change onto the bar. "You in the cavalry?"

"Yup, and getting more bowlegged every day."

"It be a hard life," agreed Jericho.

"Private Jim Clancy at your service."

"Tillison's the handle. Here, have another shot."

"I appreciate someone who hates drinking alone."

"The notion struck me, Clancy, that maybe you could help me out. The man I'm looking for is stationed at Fort Shaw. You're probably acquainted with Major Dirk Mackley?"

"So mean he'd sell his mother to the Blackfeet," snapped Jim Clancy. A frown lowered his eyelids. "You a friend of his?"

"Nope. As you said, Mackley doesn't have many friends."

The way Jericho had phrased that softened the private's eyes, and he muttered, "You bet he don't. Leastways not at Fort Shaw."

"I stopped at the fort. Was told that Mackley was

136

coming over here."

"Arcadia ain't all that big, so you shouldn't have any trouble running into the major."

Jericho puffed thoughtfully on his cigar, sent smoke scudding past the rapidly emptying bottle of whiskey and toward the back bar. "Trouble is, Mr. Clancy, I don't want him to know I'm here. Got some unfinished business that requires me having the upper hand—if you get my drift?"

"Maybe I do. So what's in it for me?"

"If you was to scout the town over and locate the major, a double eagle would buy a lot of whiskey or a run at cards."

"I dunno," the soldier said uneasily. "Maybe you're aiming to gun Major Mackley down . . ."

"If there's trouble, Mackley'll start it. I'm a peaceable man."

"Meaning you're toting that Smith and Wesson just for the hell of it." Private Jim Clancy fixed his eyes on Jericho's change, rubbed alongside his temple, downed still another glass of whiskey, and set the glass down hard. "Okay, you've got yourself a scout. Where'll you be, here?"

"Chowing down at the Turkey Trot."

The long talk with the soldier had taken Jericho's mind off his other reason for coming here. It was a different matter when he strolled outside and, moving upstreet, saw light coming from the jail. Angling across the street, he glanced in a window hoping to catch a glimpse of Marshal Brad Jericho, but on duty was an older man with a shock of coal-black hair. He picked up his gait, crossed an intersection, and entered the Turkey Trot saloon. Music and smoke bounced off the high rafters, and a woman's pleased giggle brought him gazing at a hardcase bounding after a bar girl on the staircase. The bar was to his right, but he swung the opposite way and found an empty table in the lunchroom. Washing down his meal at a back table was Sergeant MacIver, both men careful not to pay the other any particular attention. When a waitress finally came out of the kitchen and spilled water from the glass she held onto his table, Jericho cast her a tired smile and ordered the house special— Sheepherder's Scalloped Potatoes. The coffee which the waitress brought first was thick with an acrid stench, and Jericho wished he'd never left that saloon. The plate arriving a little later held him there, as did the buttermilk biscuits. He'd just ordered another plateful when the voice of Shawn MacIver froze Jericho's hand reaching for his coffee cup.

"Ah, if it isn't Marshal Jericho."

"Took the liberty of coming in the back door. Mind if I join you?"

"You're the man I came to see. Coffee?"

Jericho was seated with his back to them, and he was grateful that another couple dining close by at another table hadn't noticed the expression on his face. With a casualness he didn't feel, Jericho shifted on the chair and glanced toward the kitchen as though he had thoughts of summoning his waitress. Then he stared at his namesake, realizing right away that Brad Jericho had his mother's eyes and some of her smile. In a way, a much younger way, he resembled himself, Jericho felt. He shifted his eyes to the waitress bringing him another plate of food.

"Guess I've lost my appetite." Coming to his feet, he dropped some money on the table and headed for the barroom.

"Now ain't that a fine how-do-you-do," complained the waitress, but brightening when she saw the size of her tip.

One thought suddenly struck Lane Jericho as he found a place at the bar: he was a father. A wistful glimmer stole into his eyes. If only he had known. All he had to look back on at the moment was all those wasted years. He could have taken Laurel and the boy and started ranching, or even gotten into the sheriffing business.

"Whiskey?"

"Yup," he said wearily. He felt used up, cheated somehow.

He lingered at the bar in hopes that soldier would come back. But it was the mountie who arrived first, Shawn MacIver shouldering next to Jericho and offering to buy a round. "Well, no doubt but that the marshal of Arcadia is a troubled young man. Denied knowing anyone hereabouts selling horses to the gunrunners. I figure different. You come up with anything?"

"Got someone out looking for Major Mackley."

"You'll know where to find me if anything comes up." Sergeant MacIver swung away from the bar and passed outside.

Lane Jericho waited another half hour, then he

left to head for the boardinghouse, and upon arriving there, to hear voices coming from MacIver's room. Easing over to the closed door, he heard the voice of a woman telling of her fears for both the marshal of Arcadia and some rancher, and he rapped softly.

The door was opened by MacIver, who gestured Jericho into the room before closing the door and saying, "This is Julia Bennett. Julia's engaged to Marshal Brad Jericho. Seems there's some trouble out at her father's ranch." MacIver went on to tell of how Julia had been staying here at the boardinghouse, and of going downtown tonight and seeing him talking to Brad. "Brad Jericho talked to her afterward, told her I was a mountie here looking for gunrunners."

When his eyes shifted from MacIver to young Julia Bennett, there was a wondering expression on her face as of someone trying to recall an old acquaintance. "Nope, Miss Bennett, I'm new to these parts. Name's Con Tillison; a lawman same's MacIver, here."

"Julia, you said some men are out at your ranch buying horses."

"They've been through before, Sergeant MacIver. But that's all Pa did—sell horses to them."

"Man's got to make a living," Jericho said softly. "But we both know these aren't honest men."

"I guess . . . not."

"You ever find out what they're packing?" MacIver said.

"Maybe some long boxes? Or Gatling guns,

maybe?" Jericho chimed in.

"Yes . . . they did pack their supplies in long boxes. Kept their distance though. A—a sorry-looking lot. Pa was real worried when he sent me here. I know he's in bad trouble—but—but he's an honest man . . ."

"Did your father ever mention any names—such as Jay Paragon?"

"He's their leader. Always handled the money."

"Julia, Brad's only town marshal here. I expect he kept quiet about this so's to protect you and your father."

Blushing, she said, "I expect that's right, Marshal Tillison. And we're expecting to get married. I just can't shake this feeling I should know you." Rising from the chair, she added, "Please don't tell Brad I was here."

"We might have to, Julia," MacIver said. "For certain we'll be heading out to your father's place come morning. There's more involved here than gunrunners or your kin. Meaning war could just break out up north. This is the first real break we've had. As for John Bennett, we're hoping he'll cooperate by telling us what he knows about this. One more thing, let us talk to Brad Jericho first tomorrow morning before you see him."

After Julia Bennett had let herself out of the room, Lane Jericho fought back a yawn as he pondered over this turn of events. Tonight he felt more tired than usual, a little weak, and attributed this to the higher elevation of land the town was located on. He was kind of anxious for morning to come so he could finally confront his son.

He said, "The only reason Mackley would come here is to confer with Jay Paragon. Paragon's men must have delivered another shipment of arms to the métis. Probably heading south now by way of the Bennett ranch."

"What your drift is is that Major Mackley has received word about another arms shipment. Come morning we'll have to send a wire to Colonel De Trobriand about this. There's another thing, Jericho. Mackley brought along a patrol of around twenty men; they're bivouacked south of town. Could be that some of them are mixed up in this too."

"It's a big operation."

"It's also a puzzler Julia Bennett thinking she knew you—"

"You might as well know, Shawn, that Brad Jericho could be my son. Come morning I'll know for certain."

CHAPTER THIRTEEN

Once again the floorboards felt the thud of Major Dirk Mackley's dusty boots as he paced past Jay Paragon seated at a table with two other gunrunners and Sgt. Flin Colmar. Spread out on the table along with some bottles of whiskey and glasses and ashtrays filled with butts was a map Mackley had brought along. The windows in this large upper room in the Green Edge casino were wide open.

"I tell you, Jay, this has to be the last shipment."

"Hate to see a good thing end."

"So do I," said Mackley. "But the finger of suspicion is beginning to point Fort Shaw way. *My* way." He brought the glass to his lips and emptied it, came back to the table and pointed at the map. "A special supply train leaves the Rock Island Arsenal on the 18th—that's two weeks from now. It'll stop only to take on coal and water, at St. Paul, Miles City, probably here at Big Timber. Which is where we'll be waiting."

Crossing his legs, a cynical Jay Paragon said, "Meaning there's no guarantee it'll stop at Big Timber."

"It will," replied Mackley, "because I intend to be

on that train." He refilled his glass and let his glance shift to Sgt. Flin Colmar beginning to doze off. "So will Colmar. But I'll need some men to command."

"You brought out a patrol."

"None of those soldiers are involved in my under-cover activities. What I'll need from them are their uniforms."

Jay Paragon set down his glass as the full impli-cation of the major's statement struck home. "Seems you've got a heart of stone."

"There's nothing personal in it. You still plan on leaving in the morning?"

"Maybe."

Mackley slapped at a big blue fly clawing in on his neck, then he traced a route on the map, south-ward toward Cadotte Pass in the Rockies.

"I figure on bringing my patrol just east of the pass. You shouldn't have any trouble finding us. Just make sure that Sergeant Colmar and I are out of camp before you open fire. After your men put on those uniforms, we'll head for Miles City."

"Just whereabouts at Big Timber does that supply train take on coal and water?"

"You can't miss the water tower. As for my money, Jay, I want half of it now—the rest when we get to Big Timber."

"You've changed."

"All of us have."

Paragon shrugged as he pulled out a leather poke, and he said ruefully, "Too bad we have to end this thing."

"That's the way of it, Jay. Someday your greed's gonna be your undoing."

Glaring up at Mackley, he slid the poke across the table as the door opening into the hallway was flung open. A hardcase hurried in, then he stepped aside when two more gunrunners carried a soldier into the room and let him fall heavily to the floor. One of them said, "He was going around town looking for Major Mackley."

"I've seen him around camp," the major said. Turning he stepped to a washstand, picked up a pail of water, and dumped its contents over the unconscious man. As Pvt. Jim Clancy began to stir, the point of Mackley's boot slammed into his rib cage, and he groaned.

"All right, soldier, you've found me."

"Honest, Major Mackley," stammered Jim Clancy. "I just seen a chance to make a—a fast buck." Fear gaped open his eyes when the hardcases pulled him to his feet.

"Your knife."

The hardcase the major had spoken to passed over his hunting knife, and with a bitter smile tugging at his mouth Major Mackley drew the blade across the private's throat hard enough to draw blood.

"Please, sir," he cried out, "some gent calling himself Tillison was looking for you."

"That damned U.S. marshal's alive? You told me Black Moon had put him away!" Paragon said.

145

"Something must have gone wrong," exclaimed Mackley. On the other hand, came Mackley's angry thought, Black Moon could have headed out without trying to ambush Tillison and that mountie. The knife cut deeper. "Is Tillison here in Arcadia?"

"Yessir—upstreet at a saloon!"

"Who else was there?"

"Sir—major, sir, he was alone—I swear!"

Crinkling his mouth with a toothy grimace, Dirk Mackley slit the soldier's throat from corner to corner, backed away from the sudden spurt of blood as the gunrunners who'd been holding the man's arm let him sag downward.

"Dammit, Mackley, we could have gotten more out of him."

"He was just a messenger boy," replied Mackley as he bent over and wiped the blood off the knife on the soldier's tunic before handing it back to the hardcase. "This changes our plans. There's a possibility that Marshal Tillison could have brought some troops along. And if so, I don't want to hang around until morning. Colmar, we're heading back to camp. I suggest you leave right away, Jay."

"Half of my men are either shacking up or too damned drunk to sit a horse. Seems to me you're gettin' damned spooked over this."

"You forget, Mr. Paragon, that more than the U.S. cavalry is looking for us. Those Canadian mounties are a tenacious bunch. Or maybe we should just forget about that arms shipment?"

"No," Paragon said disgustedly. "What a hell of a

time for this to happen. But I want those weapons. All right, I'll heed your advice and vamoose out of here, tonight."

"What about him?"

"Paragon's uncaring eyes flicked from the hardcase who'd spoken to the dead soldier. "Dump him out back. Then roust the others. First we'll make tracks for the Bennett place. Mackley, you just be waiting near Cadotte Pass."

Less than an hour later, Sgt. Flin Colmar brought his horse brushing against a telegraph pole. From there he managed to stand in the saddle and cut the telegraph wire. Accompanied by Major Mackley, the sergeant passed along the eastward-running line and cut the wire a couple of more times, and then they broke for camp.

As he rode, Flin Colmar sidled wondering glances at his superior officer. It was only because of Hannah that he'd gotten involved in this gunrunning business. With the extra money he'd been able to buy her a few luxuries and take a few trips, even salt away a little nest egg. In three months his term of enlistment would be over, Colmar's plans being to entrain for the Windy City and open a saloon.

But the cold-blooded way the major had killed that soldier made Sergeant Colmar fully aware that he could be next. You didn't trust a man like Dirk Mackley. And it was too convenient for the major to have the presence of Corporal Martinsen on this patrol. Obviously the major had arranged that, and it could just be that the other two men involved, also a couple of two-stripers stationed back at Fort Shaw, were already dead. He could warn Martinsen, tell him to shag out for the Rockies. Doing so, however, would place his own life in jeopardy. A burly man with a cynical attitude, Flin Colmar knew he could take the major at fisticuffs, or weapons if it came to that. But getting back-shot was another brand of hard liquor, and so, like it or not, Colmar knew his only chance to stay alive was to let Major Dirk Mackley be bossman until they'd secured those weapons.

As they approached the fading glare of a campfire, the sound of their horses brought a shouted challenge from one of the men standing guard duty. Colmar yelled the password as they rode in.

"Yankowski, Petrie, saddle up. We're moving out." Sergeant Colmar rode his bay among the sleeping men and shouted them awake. "Any man needing more'n five hours sleep a night is a jackass. Come on, come on, hustle into them boots. Then go saddle your mounts." He swung his horse around and walked it over to Major Mackley adjusting the saddle on his horse.

"We'll head due south, Sergeant."

"Cut the military crap."

"Easy."

It was often said by those who knew him that Sergeant Colmar, a veteran of the Indian Wars, was no better'n those he'd warred against. Some claimed he'd even been a squawman, which had prompted no denials. At five-eleven, he was an inch taller and a lot bulkier than the major, while firelight revealed the contempt gleaming out of Colmar's dark brown eyes. "The way I see it, Major, is that you might try to do me in, same as Martinsen."

"Martinsen can't keep his mouth shut. And that drinking of his doesn't help either. He's perfectly capable of trying to make a deal with Colonel De Trobriand, or those lawmen. That makes him expendable."

"Suppose you're right," muttered Flin Colmar. "But from here on in we're equal partners — an equal cut right down the line. That includes what Paragon gave you back at Arcadia. Or so help me I'll tell these troopers what's in store for them."

"This is out of character, Flin. Haven't I always treated you square?"

"What you did to that soldier back at that gambling casino sort of opened my eyes." His eyes held Mackley's as he unbuttoned the flap on his service revolver and hooked his hand on the grip. "What's it gonna be, Mackley?"

"I can't make this thing work without your help, Flin." The smile only touched Dirk Mackley's eyes as he reached into a coat pocket and pulled out the leather poke. "From what I've learned, this'll be the biggest arms shipment yet. After we've pulled it off, we'll go our separate ways." He opened the poke and spilled gold nuggets into the palm of his left hand.

"Just where did Paragon come up with those nuggets?"

"I suppose from the métis. And those half-bloods probably got them from the Blackfeet. Now we have them." He handed the nuggets to Colmar.

"Maybe I should cut out now. But there'll be more money after we get those weapons."

"Catching gold fever, Sergeant?"

"Same's you . . . sir."

CHAPTER FOURTEEN

Two of them were still alive when sunlight poked a glittering hole in slumbering clouds and burned John Bennett's eyes deeper into his skull. The other man clinging to life was Marv Pelham, one of Bennett's hired hands. Strands of barbed wire bound them to corral posts, cut cruelly into their flesh, and they were hatless and vaguely aware of some gunrunners idling on the front porch of the house.

Last night the bloodletting had started, when one of them, Bo Layden, had bragged that for a silver dollar he could grease a slug into one of the waddy's ears at fifty paces. He'd done okay with Marv Pelham, slicing off the man's left ear, this while clutching a bottle of corn liquor and staggering around as he cut loose with that cumbersome Dragoon. The other hand, K.C. Allard, made the mistake of begging for mercy and trying to pull free from the barbed wire. Somewhat nettled by this, the gunrunner fired wildly before planting a killing slug in Allard's forehead.

The fun really began for the hardcases when one of the Rayburn brothers suggested they move back, with so many points for blowing away a finger, or hitting a leg or arm. Whiskey had unlocked their darker moods, those they were about to harm just empty bottles or peach cans perched on top of posts. There wasn't anything John Bennett could say to Pelham, nor did it make any difference when the gunrunners began finding the range. A shudder passed through the rancher when he got hit in the left shoulder. In rapid succession other parts of his body felt the sickening impact of lead slugs.

"Nice shot!" one gunrunner said to another as one of Pelham's fingers was torn away.

"Damned lucky is all."

"This is better'n taking out Comanches . . . or greasers."

"Tenga cuidado!" retorted a bowlegged, glowering Mex named Gomez.

His mind going into shock, John Bennett sagged deeper in the barbed wire, as Pelham had already done, and after a lonely shot rang out, the hardcases swung away and followed their lengthening shadows toward the ranch house. Their eyes still glowed with the need to inflict pain, with some of them cautiously reloading their sidearms, those who'd been drinking still holding their weapons and bragging about their marksmanship.

Along with the excruciating pain racking his body, the rancher became aware after a while of someone hunkered a few feet away. And also that it was morning, and he still clung to life. He hung limply in the barbed wire, unable to move limbs

152

shattered by leaden pellets. Somehow he felt distanced from this place, and what had happened to him. There was this great sense of fragility, and for some strange reason he felt as though he were dangling from one of those aspens rustling behind the corrals. His sins, against family and others, were many.

"Bless . . . thee . . ."

For a moment the greaser just stared up blankly at John Bennett. The serape concealed his holstered gun, that big Mexican hat shadowing his mustachioed face, and tipping it back, he said through an inquisitive smile, *"Que dijo Ud?"*

"Forgive them . . . Lord . . ." The words croaked out of John Bennett's mouth. There came to him passages from the New Testament, a kinship with the Judas of old, for was he not just as much a sinner.

"Your compadre, he awakens too." A hand dipped beneath the serape to come out grasping a bone-handled knife. Sorrowfully he added, "Senor Rancher, you should not have ordered us off your rancho."

"Kill . . . me . . ."

"That will come to pass," said the greaser, the sudden smile causing sunlight to sparkle off a gold tooth. Coming to his feet, he stepped over to Marv Pelham muttering some crazed incantation.

With all of the strength he could muster John Bennett managed to loll his head that way. And

153

now he wished he hadn't, a sickness passing through his body when the greaser began slicing away the cowpuncher's thinning rusty locks. The scream broke out deep in John Bennett's innards. It tore past his windpipe to rip out in a frightful agonizing wail that got the horses milling about in the corrals and set men's teeth on edge. His mind snapping, the rancher descended into a pit of madness as he died.

Unmindful of it all, Gomez kept working away at the scalp lock, pausing only when one of those standing guard called out that riders were coming in. Then the hair came loose from the bloody scalp and he set it on a corral pole to dry. While pawing through the waddy's pocket, Gomez realized that the man was dead, which only provoked an indifferent shrug as he stepped over to see what he could find in the rancher's pockets.

While most of the gunrunners brought their mounts over to the corrals, Jay Paragon drew up by the ranch house and told one of the idlers to rustle up some grub.

"There's hot coffee."

"That'll do for now."

"Something happen back at Arcadia?"

"We'll gather up the horses, leave around noon."

"Jay," said Sid Rayburn as he swung down, "Check that out—"

Paragon swung his attention to the three dead men and the greaser slinking away, realized that he should have expected something like this. Anyway, he mused tiredly, it hadn't been their policy to leave witnesses behind. There would be other ranchers willing to sell their horses, and when one of the hardcases inquired about the bodies, Paragon said, "Leave them. Rayburn, you and Driscoll and I'll chow down in the house. Got something to discuss. You, tend to our horses."

Tramping through the living room into the kitchen, the gunrunners dropped onto wooden chairs as the hardcase tending the stove brought over three cups and a blackened coffeepot. Filling their cups, he swung back and set the pot down and dropped a hunk of slab bacon in a frying pan. The others grimaced away the bitter taste of the coffee as Jay Paragon spoke.

"One bunch'll take the horses and head them into that valley between the Big and Little Belt mountains. Hold them at that abandoned army camp. "This'll be your job, Rayburn."

"No problem handling that chore. Leaving town the way we did sure raises hell with a man's sleep."

"I think the major was just blowing smoke."

"About those lawmen bringing some soldiers along. Tom, a little caution goes a long ways to keepin' a man alive."

"Guess so. Leastways, we're still keepin' clear of the law. Damn, Jay, I hate to see this thing end. Another three months of running guns and I'd have clear title to a spread down in Wyoming."

155

"All of us have made some easy money," said Paragon. "And I see no problem in getting rid of those soldiers."

"Mackley's a sly one," said Driscoll. "He could be some kind of hero if he turns us in."

"Along with being foxy as hell, Mackley's no fool. Meaning he ain't looking to get a medal pinned on his chest. Big Timber will be the last we'll see of Major Dirk Mackley. Then he'll be just another army deserter. Nope, I don't trust him; sooner nestle up to a sidewinder. But don't worry, boys, there'll always be others like Mackley wanting to make some easy money. Soon's you've chowed up, Tom, pick out those who'll be going with us to rendezvous with Mackley—the best shots."

"Sure, Jay. Been thinking of how badly some of them Blackfeet want to join up with the métis and hit the war trail up in Canady."

"Louis Riel don't know it but the price of weapons has gone up considerable."

"Think he'll pay?"

Jay Paragon laughed mirthlessly as a plate was slid before him on the cluttered table, and he said, "Someday all of us will pay for dealing with the Devil—be you an Injun, half-blood, or outlaw such as us."

CHAPTER FIFTEEN

A day before, Louis Riel and his métis had departed from the Blackfoot encampment on the Teton River. Only a handful of half-bloods had stayed behind, with these métis, aware now of Red Cloud's anger, staying in their own camp a couple of miles downriver.

Dawning was a painful time for the elderly chief, some of his discomfort from the lingering effects of an arrow wound, but mostly from the rigors of gout and rheumatism, though medicine men had claimed to have cast out the demons causing these diseases. He had not told them of a visit to a Canadian army doctor. To have done so would have brought down their wrath. Gathering the robe around him, Red Cloud sat down by the pine-scented fire passing up smoke through a hole in the tepee, drew up his legs as a squaw handed him a cup of broth—a mixture of herbs and dog meat and fatty gristle. He savored it while seeking some sign in the wavy tendrils of smoke, anything that would give him, guidance to the festering problems

157

caused by Running Elk and Kills Two. The sub-chiefs and many of their followers had trailed after the métis. It was not easy, he realized, to quit the warring ways. Now Red Cloud had no choice but to gather those who'd stayed behind, Bloods, Piegans, Blackfeet, and head after the malcontents. He hated to see Blackfeet spill one another's blood. But he was grimly aware that both the pony soldiers and the Canadian soldiers would like nothing better than doing to the Blackfoot what they'd already done to the Sioux and other Indian tribes.

With the help of a squaw, Red Cloud donned his war regalia, and he was reaching for his old Winchester repeating rifle when the guttural voice of Wolfskin Man pierced through the open tent flap. Crouching to get outside, he found a warrior being handed the reins of his war pony, and a vast contingent of other warriors, some already there on their ponies, others radiating toward Red Cloud's lodge from all quarters of the large encampment. Distantly, squaws and children hovered by their tepees.

"Some of your brothers have already left with the métis." The summery wind carried his words to the others, but he was more aware of their indecision, knowing that he would be too old to travel with them. "It is the métis who want war. If the Blackfoot Nation enters into this foolishness, the white men could seek their revenge by taking away our ancestral lands. This is a war neither métis nor the Blackfeet can win. Not even the ghost dance can bring the buffalo back. Running Elk knows this, as does Kills Two. By going with the métis they have placed all of us in danger. But there is still time to go after them . . . to try to reason with our brothers."

"Our chief is right."

"But if we agree to go," said another, "to keep our brothers from joining the métis in their rebellion, it must be made clear to the Americans, the Canadians, that no longer will white settlers be allowed to pass onto our lands."

"There is wisdom in your words, Wild Gun." Oftentimes, pondering Red Cloud, Wild Gun, one of the younger chiefs, had come to him for counsel. And that Wild Gun and most of the other chiefs were here, spoke well for Red Cloud's prestige among his people. Nevertheless it was time to let another be in charge as they sought to overtake the other Blackfeet under Running Elk and Kills Two.

Once he was aboard his horse, Red Cloud called out, "It is time for Wild Gun to be the war chief of his people. So, my friend, show us what to do this day."

Startled by the old chief's proclamation, the Blood's eyes registered his surprise, and then Wild Gun, a tall, sinewy man, vaulted into the saddle and rode over to Red Cloud, where he wheeled his war pony around and surveyed the gathering.

"This is an unexpected honor," he said. "One not

to be taken lightly. However, some of you must stay here and guard the camp. For we ride not to make war. We ride to bring back those who have rebelled against the wishes of our great council."

CHAPTER SIXTEEN

"You'll oblige me by elevating your hands!"

The last thing Lane Jericho expected was to be arrested by the marshal of Arcadia. In the uncertain glow of lantern light he could see one deputy hovering by an open side door, at least two more easing in by the open back door, with Marshal Brad Jericho striding boldly toward him. For want of anything better to do Lane hoisted the saddle he'd just picked up onto the back of the canelo, then he framed a smile and raised his arms.

"Seems the law gets up awful early around here."

"It does."

"What am I being charged with?"

"Suspicion of murder in the first degree!"

"Thought there was only one kind. Mighty heavy words."

"You've got all the earmarks of a gunhand."

"Since when"—he shrugged with his shoulders—"is packing a gun a crime?"

"Want me to take him down a couple of pegs, Brad?"

"Just watch him, Leggert." Marshal Brad Jericho reached out and eased Lane's six-gun out of its holster. Then he stepped behind Lane and patted his clothes down in search of a hideout gun. Close like this, he took a hard look at the man he'd just arrested. "You drifted through here before, mister?"

"Not that I recollect."

"But you do recollect your name?"

Here it was, deliberated Lane Jericho, tell the marshal just who he was, or by coining some alias, leave his past alone. The boy even had some of his mannerisms, along with those eyes that all at once brought Laurel into the immediate present. Even the gun Marshal Brad Jericho was gripping, a .45 Peacemaker, spoke of his having some horse sense. But one wrong move on his part could see it spouting flame.

"Who am I supposed to have killed, some local?" he said.

"Last night you were seen talking to Corp. Jim Clancy. Matter of fact, the barkeep who I talked to will swear an oath that your conversation with the corporal became awful interesting."

"Reckon I did have a few words with the corporal. But did this bardog mention that Corporal Clancy was in good health when he departed from that saloon?"

"Makes no difference now, since Clancy's dead. Among the bullets that did him in, Corporal Clancy had the hell beat out of him. What did

162

you use, mister, crowbar?"

Lane could tell from the way the deputies were closing in that he had little chance of getting away. And just where was a Canadian mountie when you needed one? He expected Shawn MacIver to show up at any minute. Since he was also the unknown quantity, Lane knew that merely showing the U.S. marshal's badge he toted would carry no weight with the marshal of Arcadia. Henceforth, if he announced himself to these town lawmen as one of them, upholder of the law Con Tillison, that should suffice to see the name Lane Jericho buried untidily in the local cemetery. There was another name to consider at the moment—Julia Bennett. Her presence last night at Mrs. Magstadt's boardinghouse, meals extra, the grim contents of Julia's statement that gunrunners were lurking out at her pa's ranch, could not only trigger off Marshal Brad Jericho's Peacemaker but his temper. Being caught between these deputies and a hard place displeased Lane mightily. So a gambler's instinct came to the fore.

"I came here, Marshal, to try my luck at games of chance. Since the corporal was busted—and that bardog can attest to that—I recruited Corporal Clancy to scout out some places of action. To get to the gist of it, Clancy never came back. I told him we'd rendezvous at the Turkey Trot saloon. Tiring of waiting, I trudged back to my room."

After checking the brand on Lane's horse, Deputy Leggert said, "Where'd you steal the horse, mister?"

"Probably the same place you got to be so ugly."

The deputy pivoted and slammed his crooked elbow into Lane Jericho's lower back, and Lane gasped as he dropped to his knees. "Where'd you steal it?" he repeated.

"He's its rightful owner," stated Shawn MacIver. He shoved past one of the deputies and strode along the runway. "What's the problem here?"

Throwing his deputy an angry glance, Marshal Brad Jericho said, "We have reason to hold him. For murder."

"That's hitting the nail right on the head, Marshal," said MacIver. "A lot of outlaws have tried standing up to this man."

"This was a soldier. Out of Fort Shaw. We found his body in an alley."

"Would that be a corporal name of Jim Clancy?"

"It is."

"First of all you've arrested a U.S. marshal. Gents, this here's Con Tillison. We're trying to find some gunrunners."

Struggling to his feet, Lane placed a steadying hand on a stall wall. He looked at Brad Jericho. "I'd admire to have my gun back. There's little doubt that some gunrunners have been hanging around Arcadia, and that they killed Corporal Clancy."

"Which is why we'd like a private word with you," MacIver said.

"Sure," Brad Jericho said edgily. "Go chow down, men. One thing, Leggert, don't ever try a stunt like that again. You got that?" A tight smile on his lips, he handed the Smith & Wesson back to Lane, then as his deputies trailed out of the livery stable, he followed Lane and MacIver into a small room the hostler used as an office. Short boards had been placed over empty nail kegs to pass as chairs and there was a rickety rolltop desk before which sat a padded rocking chair, which MacIver claimed.

"No sense tracking through the brush, Marshal Jericho; haven't got the time for that. Julia Bennett called on us last night. Told us about the situation out at her pa's ranch. You know he's been dealing with these gunrunners." MacIver waited until Lane and Brad Jericho had found seats, then he added, "You've been protecting him because of the girl."

"Perhaps. Anyway, what happens outside of the town limits is no concern of mine," Brad said flatly.

"I doubt if you want your future father-in-law getting himself killed," Lane threw in. "Those gunrunners killed that soldier. And I found out they left town late last night. Probably beelining out to the Bennett place, where they'll pick up some horses and head south. You also know that Major Dirk Mackley is in town."

"He's discussing civic matters with the town council."

"That may be," MacIver said. "But it's our opinion the major has been making a deal with Jay Paragon's gunrunners."

"Well, Major Mackley was here. Was told he pulled out of town too."

"Damn," spat out the mountie, "I don't like the smell of this. Paragon has a habit of not leaving witnesses behind. That rancher, John Bennett, was useful to Paragon as long as he had need for fresh horses. It's my opinion they're making one final run south to steal some weapons. Then head north and sell them to the métis."

"That means," said Lane, "getting to the Bennett place as quickly as possible. Marshal, will you help us?"

"Reckon I don't have any choice. Sure, count me and my deputies into this. Can't say the same for the townfolk."

The bronze bell clanging in the fire hall tower brought townspeople converging on the main street. A smoldering match discarded by a careless outlaw or drunk or chimney sparks had often caused chain fires in towns composed of wooden buildings. Instead of a fire, they found their town marshal waving them over to the jail.

"Doggonit, Marshal Jericho, you just broke a city ordinance by sounding that bell."

"Can't be helped. Hey you, Leggert, herd those folks over here."

Behind the marshal and under the shade of the porch stood Lane and Sergeant MacIver, with Lane Jericho feeling out of sorts because of the badge pinned to his shirt. Dust was swirling along the hard-packed street, the northerly wind picking up more as it began warming into the seventies, and tugging at the canvas awning in front of Goody's Mercantile Store. Sprinkled among the onlookers were a few outlaws, con men and gamblers, bawdyhouse girls. A path began clearing for Mayor Frank Masad trailed by Joshua Yeager and another member of the town council. Masad, portly with leonine features, had on a blue satin vest over a starched shirt, and he was dabbing at his forehead with a checkered bandanna while fending off those wanting to know the reason for this get-together.

"Folks, I'm sure the marshal can explain this." He dipped his hat to a couple of bustled, tight-waisted women, which provoked some laughter, then he was confronting Marshal Jericho. "This better be good."

"Is murder a good enough reason?"

In a whispery voice the mayor said, "You mean that soldier?"

"He breathed the same air you did."

"Why . . . of course it'll have to be investigated. But—but to scare the town half to death by ringing the fire bell . . ."

"Didn't mean, Your Honor, to take you away from that pinochle game."

Shawn MacIver eased away from the jail wall, came to stand alongside the marshal of Arcadia, drew himself erect as his eyes swept from Mayor Masad to the restless crowd. His first venture here had seen the mountie getting together with the town council, the purpose being to gain their support in his search for those supplying arms to the métis. All he'd gotten were a few rebuffs, some half-hearted promises from the law-abiding citizens of this frontier town, a warning that too many lawmen could drive their best customers away. Which could only mean the outlaws.

"To clear the air, and more or less absolve your marshal of any blame, I requested that he summon the citizenry here." The smile radiated MacIver's concern for those he was addressing. "I have had the pleasure of meeting your most capable mayor and members of your town council. This on a previous visit to the garden of Montana—which could only be the gallant city of Arcadia. Permit me to introduce myself, if you will. I'm Sergeant Shawn MacIver of the Royal Canadian Mounted Police. My purpose in being here is to find those who've been selling arms to some renegades. Sadly enough, a soldier from Fort Shaw was killed by these men. Now these killers are heading out to do harm to one of your neighbors. Most certainly you all know John Bennett."

"Deals in horses."

"Clannish as hell, though."

"We'll be needing some able to handle a sidearm or rifle to form a posse," broke in Brad Jericho.

"You got any proof these men killed that soldier?"

MacIver glanced at the mayor of Arcadia. "We're fairly certain they did."

"Fairly certain is a far piece from hard evidence."

Merchant Joshua Yeager stepped forward. "We don't have a county sheriff. But I see one of you is packing a U.S. marshal's badge. So I believe that going after these outlaws comes under his bailiwick."

Lane groaned inwardly. He brought the boot that had been braced against the wall down and tugged his hat lower over his eyes. About the people clustered out in the street was a sullenness, a grim refusal to believe the oratory of Sergeant MacIver, for forming a posse would be a signal to the outlaw element that Arcadia had turned against them. In a way, the merchants and a lot of the townspeople were no better than the outlaws they catered to, overpricing merchandise and letting a lot of other undesirables drift in. There was one church, Lane had noticed, but he doubted that many attended it regularly. Now they began breaking away, by ones or twos, then in larger bunches, with the mayor shaking his head.

"Can't say as I blame them," the mayor said.

"You didn't help much," Brad said accusingly.

"Perhaps your only concern for Bennett is that you're courting his daughter."

The frustration and anger that had been building in Brad Jericho caused him to grab the mayor's big flowery tie, but MacIver was there to hold back the marshal's right hand.

"Easy, lad," he said calmly. "Easy. Just for the record, Your Honor, it's perfectly legal for Marshal Con Tillison to declare martial law—have your bastion of lawlessness overrun with cavalry. Unfortunately, the men we want are gone. I can neither pity nor do I want to be a part of this horrible place. Because sooner or later the scavengers you're catering to just might exact a terrible price." Releasing Brad's arm, he smiled at the younger man. "Now, lad, the question is whether your jurisdiction extends out as far as the Bennett ranch."

"Let's ride!"

CHAPTER SEVENTEEN

The shock of what he was viewing sparkled in Brad Jericho's eyes, held him saddlebound and trying to figure out a reason for such terrible brutality.

"They just . . . left them there."

"They'll be buried properly," said Shawn MacIver as he glanced at Lane Jericho loping in past the barn.

The canelo sidestepped away from the stench of death as Lane drew up by the corral. "Near as I can gather, one bunch left with the horses. But most of the gunrunners took off more to the southwest."

"How much of a head start do they have?"

"Three, four hours."

Swinging down, the mountie checked the position of the afternoon sun. From there he turned to look at a grassy knoll north of the buildings where a few cattle were grazing on little bluestem and needlegrass sprinkled with bell-shaped prairie larkspur. The view held him, as did the jagged peaks holding captive this peaceful valley. Up north in Saskatchewan it was more open country, though here was a place a man could come to like. Now murder had been done, and with a wry grimace on his face, MacIver watched one of the deputies come out of a shed carrying two round-nosed spades. MacIver's suggestion that there might be more shovels in the barn caused a deputy to head that way.

"There's a couple of horses in the barn." Dutch Leggert said. "I'll throw a harness on one and hitch it to that wagon." And he too ambled toward the barn.

Dismounting, Lane assisted in the grim task of removing the barbed wire from the dead bodies. Then they were wrapped in blankets found in the house and placed in the wagon. Lane turned to the mountie. "You're the expert on those gunrunners."

"Obviously they're going after more weapons. Major Mackley tipped them off to another arms shipment."

"Probably why they cut the telegraph line back at Arcadia."

"Exactly. An arms shipment by the military out west will be done by rail. Back at Fort Shaw the only man privy to this information besides the commandant would of course be Mackley."

Leading a horse up to the wagon, Leggert

hooked it to the traces and climbed up to ease down on the wide wagon seat. The others fell silent, falling in behind, and with Brad Jericho filled with the dread of what he'd have to tell Julia Bennett.

Quietly Shawn MacIver said, "Right about now Major Mackley is leading the soldiers under his command in that general direction." His eyes shifted to the southwest. "And why? To utilize their uniforms after those gunrunners ambush them. Then it'll be Major Dirk Mackley leading a bunch of gunrunners masquerading as soldiers down to intercept that arms shipment. Nice and tidy, isn't it, Marshal Tillison?"

"So far everything's gone Mackley's way. And too damned bad those gunrunners have such a head start, Shawn."

"It is, but as civilized men we must do the right thing and give these men a Christian burial."

Under a cloudy sky the bodies were lowered into the ground and then covered up with red-loamy soil. Knowing they would have to leave right away, no wooden crosses had been made, but MacIver had fetched along a small pocket Bible, the King James version, and its presence in the man's large blocky hands caused everyone to remove their hats. Heads were lowered and eyes watched silver-tinted digger bees puzzle over the upturned soil of a hive suddenly dislodged as Ser-

173

geant MacIver thumbed open the Bible to a page notched before — the Twenty-third Psalm. The flitting passage of a sleepy orange butterfly over the gravesite made them shift their booted feet somewhat, with the chiding words recited to them by MacIver urging them to get on the move. Other words held them gravebound.

"He was a minister."

Closing the Bible, MacIver said, "Mr. Bennett?"

"Some time ago," Brad Jericho went on. "Back east or south someplace, Julia told me. Just got off that gospel road. Never could quite get a grip on himself — or the ranch. But laid to rest like this under these aspens, maybe John Bennett's found peace at last."

Donning his hat, Lane said, "Time's a-wasting. I figure we've got to split up."

"Which means, Marshal Jericho," said MacIver, "sending your deputies after those stolen horses. This is, unless you'd rather head back to Arcadia."

"Been planning to hand in my badge," said Brad. "Now things are different. Leggert, we'll try to hook up with you later. All we're asking is that you track them down, then wait for us."

"I wasn't planning on jumping them." Then Leggert and the other deputies swung aboard their horses and headed out.

Back at the corrals, MacIver said, "Paragon has gotten himself a small army. All we can do is follow them, hope we run across a telegraph line someplace. Then get word to the military."

"There'll be no lines where those gunrunners are headed," said Lane. "I figure they'll be moving fast. Careful enough to keep an eye fixed to their backtrail."

"Except for a few ranches," Brad said, "this is unsettled country." He brought his horse into motion, rode with the others past the ranch buildings and followed Lane picking up the trail of Jay Paragon and his gunrunners. "It was me, I'd head them stolen horses into the Smith River valley. Which is the natural gateway down to the Northern Pacific's main line. Another place down there that could draw them in is White Sulphur Springs."

"Yes," MacIver said, "I've heard some of my friends tell about those mineral springs. Splendid accommodations for the genteel. Wouldn't mind having a go at the place myself."

All during the brief burial ceremonies Lane had felt the hostile eyes of Dutch Leggert on him. Something was bothering the man. It was entirely possible that Leggert could be on Jay Paragon's payroll. Another thing that bothered him was Brad having the man for a deputy.

"Did you inherit Dutch Leggert or hire him on?" Lane asked Brad.

"He was a fixture when they hired me. Why'd you ask?"

"The natural curiosity of a star packer." He glanced at MacIver spurring ahead.

"Can't shake this feeling we should know one another, Marshal Tillison."

Then a wave from MacIver caused both men to canter their horses across a swampy area marked by a small greenish pond, and with Brad Jericho still troubled by his inability to place where he'd seen Lane before. Forgotten was his wallet stowed in a saddlebag, for inside it was a fading picture of his parents, because it had no connection to a man calling himself a U.S. marshal. The tainted picture his mother had painted of Lane Jericho told of gambling and six-gun showdowns. It puzzled him, after all these years, that Laurel could still talk fondly of his father.

It took the greater shank of the afternoon to work out of the valley and strike toward the limestone ridges and humpbacked hills that formed a natural barrier to the Rockies looming ever taller. Along the way they came across drifting cattle and wild horses, and game was plentiful. Fearing an ambush, they'd spread out more. There was more timber now in the upward thrust of the land. Not too long ago, Lane pondered, this higher elevation would have sapped his strength, left him fighting for air, but still he welcomed the occasional stops they'd made.

"Yonder, the gap between those mountains is Cadotte Pass." Brad reined up his horse on a rocky ledge, swung his arm in a southerly direction. "That wide, meandering cut beyond those hills is the Missouri River."

MacIver shifted his eyes to fresh hoofprints passing down a break in the ledge. "I make out that we're still about a half day behind them. Anyway, it's coming onto night. There seems to be a creek down among those pines."

"Maybe we should press on."

"I hate doing so on a tired horse." said MacIver.

"And we could lose their trail," agreed Lane.

Grimacing, Brad said, "No sense arguing about it. We'll camp yonder then. Give me a chance to catch some trout."

They set up their camp in a small meadow hemmed in by pine trees and close to the bank of a swift-running stream. Sprinkled among the lush grass were mountain flowers. For a while alpenglow radiated down from the mountains, their campfire now their only light, the heat of day quickly extinguished by a night chill. While the coffeepot warmed over the hot flames, Lane hunkered close to it, nearby was MacIver tamping tobacco into the bowl of his briar pipe, and just upstream Brad Jericho's fishing pole bowed as another trout found his baited hook.

"Spent many a lonesome night camped out up in the province. It's the solitude that works on a man. You become part of the wilderness. Dream grand dreams."

"What does your wife think of your being a mountie?"

"Could have gotten married, once, but after a while I got over that idea. Isn't it about time you had a father and son talk?"

"Don't push me." Wrapping one of his gloves around the handle of the coffeepot, Lane filled their cups.

"The way he's been eying you, Mr. Jericho, makes me believe it won't be too long before he figures it out."

"Shawn," Lane questioned, "just what in blazes do I tell the . . . boy? Got nothing of a personal nature to prove out who I am. We're more or less strangers, just some lawmen who got thrown together."

"What was her name?"

"Laurel—kind of painful thinking about her again. Don't even know if she's still alive."

"You've got all the earmarks of being a born worrier. Chances are, Lane, she loved you, told your son about the places you lived, the people you knew. My opinion is that you're a lucky man."

"How's that?"

MacIver's pipe pointed toward the creek. "Was me, I'd be proud of having a son like that."

"Can't argue with that. It's just . . . that I have to build up a little more grit before I tackle that chore. Not to change the subject, but we could be wrong about Major Mackley."

"We could. But I doubt it."

The horses picked it up first and started whickering, and then Lane and MacIver caught the distant rattling of gunfire echoing in from the southwest. Brad Jericho stopped cutting up the fish he'd caught, let his questioning eyes go to the others.

"Guess you were a hundred proof right about Major Mackley," Lane said quietly. "His men never had a chance."

"We could saddle up and hightail it down there."

"Hightail it where?" said MacIver as the gunfire died away. "There's nothing we can do for those soldiers now. And about all we'll do is head out and get lost ourselves." Removing his hat, he rubbed a hand along his hairline, the chiseled planes of his face telling how he felt at the moment. "No," he added in a softer tone of voice, "morning'll come early enough. My belly is rubbing against my backbone—so are yours. I'll rustle out my frying pan and some lard, some beans." Shoving to his feet, he stepped over to his saddlebags.

"Don't worry, Brad, we'll catch up with them killers."

"All I want is Mackley and that Paragon in my gunsights."

"You ever killed anyone before?"

"There's always a first time!" he said hotly.

Lane dumped the grounds out of his tin cup and eyed the younger man, and he said chidingly, "Felt the same way a long time ago. I was just a working cowhand, down around Abilene. One Saturday night me and Rusty Keene rode into town flushed with a month's wages. Rusty always had the notion he was better'n most at gambling. It proved different when he lost his wages in a crooked game. To a gunslick name of Faraday. So he made the mistake of asking Faraday to take a stroll out back of that gambling casino. Which was where Faraday's partner tore a hole in Rusty's backside with a Greener. Having somewhat of a hot temper myself, I took off after those who'd killed Rusty. Caught up with them at Diablo . . . took both of them out. Afterward, had to live with what I'd done. There were a lot of sleepless nights, along with me having to get used to the rep of a fast gun pinned on me."

"Texas, you said?"

"Texas."

"That was where my mother met this gambler she married—some no-account named Jericho. Ever run into him?"

"Texas is a whole country," murmured Lane. Strong in him was the temptation to take Brad aside, get this thing settled. To find out if Laurel was still alive.

180

"You gonna tell him or not?"

Lane pivoted around and said to the mountie, "Let it lay."

"Tell me what?"

"That morning'll come damned early." Lane stepped away from the firelight and unrolled his bedroll.

And Brad Jericho said questioningly, "Tillison, you're right about that quick temper of yours." Then he glanced at MacIver striding away to check on the horses. Scowling to himself, Brad veered over and slumped down by his saddle. He resented Tillison telling how it felt to kill a man. That came with being a town marshal, especially in a place like Arcadia. He took off his hat and hooked it on a knee and reached for the makings.

As he shaped a cigarette, Brad's eyes wandered skyward. It was Julia Bennett who'd pointed out the various star formations. "When we're apart," Julia had told him, "fix your eyes upon the Seven Sisters, in the shoulder of Taurus, the Bull, as I'll be doing. Somehow I'll know you're thinking about me."

"Whereabouts are those stars?"

"There," she'd pointed out.

"How come you know so much about the night sky?"

"Books and such. And what an Indian told me about them."

"Just what Indians do you know?"

"Sometimes they pass by our ranch. The Blackfeet Indians believe that every star was once a human being, and that when a person dies, his spirit rises to the heavens and becomes a new star. One of their legends tells how the North Star came to be. The Morning Star came to earth and chose an Indian girl as his bride. He took her back to the heavens, where they lived happily. His wife was allowed to do almost anything she wanted, but was warned against digging a certain turnip. She disobeyed, and the turnip she pulled up made a hole in the heavens. She was returned to the earth and her child became a star that was used to fill up the hole that she had made. This star child must always stay in place to fill the hole, and can never move about as the others do. And that is why the North Star never moves, according to Blackfoot legend."

"Oh, Julia, it's my fault your father got killed," he uttered softly. "I . . . I should have stepped in before . . . warned him about those gunrunners." He sat there long after the others had sought their bedrolls. Before stumbling into Arcadia, well, there'd been one cowtown after another, and places like Denver or Cheyenne. Brief stays that hadn't allowed young Brad Jericho to make many friends. They'd parted at Bozeman, Laurel Jericho taking up residence there, and her only son on the move again.

He couldn't go back to Arcadia and face Julia.

For the blood of her father and his men were on Brad's hands. As for Marshal Con Tillison, he'd show the lawman he could kill too, and have no remorse afterward.

CHAPTER EIGHTEEN

Jay Paragon backed away from the man he'd just hammered to the ground. After a while the gunrunner managed to roll over onto his back. He hacked blood and a broken piece of tooth out of his mouth, the fear written plain on his face that Paragon might still unsheath his sidearm.

"You others—you'll do as I say!" The reason for Paragon's outburst of violence had been the hardcase wanting to use his double-rigged Texas saddle instead of the regulation army issue, which until late last night had belonged to Corporal Martinsen. His naked body, and that of the other soldiers, lay where they'd fallen further upstream. Warming sunlight poked through screening cottonwoods, and in their branches jays were singing as they flitted about.

Paragon went on, "Now that you've shaved and trimmed your hair, try to act and ride like cavalrymen. No telling who you might run into

184

on the way to Miles City. Just remember, Mackley's in command. You'll take orders from him and Sergeant Colmar and like it."

Flexing the bruised knuckles of his left hand, Paragon turned his back on the hardcase shoving up from the ground and walked up to Mackley seated on his horse. "The money they'll be getting out of this should keep them in line. Anyone gives you any guff, gun him down."

"At least they can ride and handle a gun," Mackley said cynically. "I have to be in Miles City in exactly one week. A little recruit training along the way should whip them into shape."

"I like the way we've got this planned."

"Just be waiting at Big Timber."

"Trust me, Dirk. How many years have we been . . . partners?"

"Too damned many," he said sullenly. "And I'll want the rest of my money when I get to Big Timber."

"It'll be there. Been thinking, Dirk. Don't I recollect one of those soldiers we killed last night as working for you back at Fort Shaw?"

"Martinsen had become a liability. Drank too much, which means he couldn't be trusted to keep quiet about this."

"Just wondering."

"Consider this, Jay. That Martinsen could have told them about you too. I did you a favor by bringing him along."

Grinning, Paragon said, "Dirk, I always could

185

count on you. Adios, partner."

Around a quick glare Major Dirk Mackley reined ahead and pulled up alongside Sergeant Colmar, the sergeant barking at the fifteen gunrunners masquerading as soldiers to move out. For a while they followed the creek, then forded it and struck toward the northern reaches of the Little Belts, beyond which lay Lewistown and the main road heading down to Miles City. Jay Paragon, along with the extra horses and two dozen gunrunners set out on a more southerly route. Their hasty departure from Arcadia had prevented them from stocking up on whiskey and food staples. But it was Paragon's intention to borrow what he could at any ranch they might encounter. They went at a canter at times, then would walk their horses, and around noon while passing through a draw, water trickling from a rocky crevice brought them over. At the base of the slope a large pond caused them to dismount.

"How much farther to that army camp?" a hardcase grumbled.

"First we have to work our way around the Big Belts, Willard. Sobering up too hard on your system?"

"For damned sure it don't help my disposition none."

Paragon, who'd knelt down to refill his canteen, said, "A couple of you, Towner and Bladsoe, ride up on that mesa and see if anything's back there."

"Soldiers, you mean?"

"I ain't a-looking for someone from the Salvation Army. It'll either be cavalry or those lawmen. Now, get."

And Jay Paragon had cause to worry, for easing into that camp just to the east of Cadotte Pass were the Jerichos and Shawn MacIver. They scared up vultures picking at the dead bodies. This unsettled Brad Jericho so much he unlimbered his handgun and cut loose at a couple of turkey vultures taking their own sweet time about getting airborne. Though he caused a few feathers to flutter away from the vultures sweeping over the treeline, they caught a rising current of summery air and soared toward the clouds.

"Not only is that terrible shooting," yelled MacIver, "but you might have warned those gunrunners. Leather that gun."

Lane Jericho swung down and ground-hitched his reins. The wind moaned through the cottonwoods, carrying with it the sweet smell of rain. Lane studied the immediate terrain. Just to the north stood a red-clayey bluff scoured by the weather and broken in places by sunken recesses large enough to ride a horse into.

"Once we leave, those vultures'll pick the bodies clean."

"It'd take too long to bury them."

"Yonder, those caves. We can stack them in one of the caves and block the opening best we can. Later we can tell the U.S. Army where to find the bodies."

"They deserve that much," agreed MacIver.

"It's fixin' to rain," said Brad.

"This country needs it bad," Lane responded.

"Ah—" said MacIver, hesitating as he'd been just about to call out Lane's real name, "Tillison, maybe you'd better scout out where they went. My guess is that Mackley took some men and headed downstream."

"Yup, there'll be two trails." Climbing into the saddle, Lane added, "I figure Paragon to hook up with those who left earlier with those stolen horses." He spurred away.

"Well, lad, I guess it's you and me left to do some manual labor. Fortunately, it's only a few rods to that cave." And after they'd carried a third of those who'd been killed into the cave, both men paused to remove their coats, and have a sip of water. Every so often one or two vultures would glide in but wheel away, upon spotting Brad and MacIver and their horses switching their tails under the cottonwoods. When the last body was stretched out in the cave, they covered the entrance with underbrush and rolled nearby rocks there too, an effective barricade for now, but after a while the stench from the bloating bodies would bring in coyote and other game animals. Back at the creek, MacIver slumped down and untied the bandanna from around his neck.

"I don't know what to make of Con Tillison,"

Brad commented.

"He's a different breed, all right."

"Know I've run into him before."

"Could be, since U.S. marshals move around a lot. Promise me that you won't make any reckless moves when we catch up to these men."

"I'm no kid. I can handle myself."

"It is more a question of holding in your anger, Brad. Men who can't do that generally wind up dead. I'd hate to see that happen to you, lad."

Southeasterly in the Smith River valley the three deputies from Arcadia had stopped to put on their rain slickers. Clouds lay under the peaks hemming in the sloping valley, with the freshening wind whipping rain around the horsemen. A violent thunderclap brought Dutch Leggert's horse backing around, and he grabbed the reins and swore.

"Easy, you ugly bronc!"

Arlo Goddard, a lanky man packing a D. Moore .38 rimfire, settled aboard his horse and said, "It just don't figure them making no attempt to hide their backtrail. 'Cause the way these tracks are heading, it's a sure bet these outlaws are making for that old army camp."

"Arlo, you worry too much," said Leggert. "One thing I hate is riding in wet weather."

"I've been watching you, Dutch."

Placing a spurred boot in a stirrup, Leggert found his saddle as he scowled at the other deputy, a former Jawkawker named Ray Madden, and Leggert retorted, "Why's that?"

"All you seem concerned about is our backtrail. Expecting someone?"

"It could be, Madden, that these outlaws left a few behind to get at us. I know what's in front of us — nothing but creeks and dry washes and empty valley. A couple of men with rifles could pick us off real slick if we was to get careless. Well?"

"You're in charge."

"Just remember that, dammit. C'mon, might's well follow this trail afore the rain washes it away."

Under a lowering and gray sky the deputies loped their mounts through a dry wash showing puddles of rain water. The rain came down harder, blowing in vague sheets, and the Smith River was there before any of them realized it, with Leggert in the lead and pulling back sharply on his reins to keep from piling over a crumbly bank. He veered to his right and kept on the move, craving a cigarette, but mostly a place to get out of the weather. No longer were there any hoofmarks to follow, and if the others could have seen the stony set to Dutch Leggert's face, they would have changed their minds about following the man. Then it was Leggert's upraised arm that brought them loping up to either side.

"Appears to be Camp Baker—beyond those trees a half mile or so."

"Don't see anything? Just some run-down buildings."

"Did you expect to, Madden? What's it gonna be, boys?"

"We was told to wait for the others, Dutch. You ain't thinking of going in there, are you? There must be a dozen or so of them gunrunners."

"No guts, no glory, Arlo."

"Glory ain't enough on what I get paid."

"Figure it out," said Leggert. "We ain't wearin' no badges. Just three cowpokes seekin' a place to get out of this damnable rain. These gunrunners believe that U.S. marshal brought along some soldiers. So they'll pretty much tell us to hightail it out instead of startin' anything."

"Don't sound too bad."

"Could use some coffee and a roof over my head."

"Just let me do the talkin'." Dutch Leggert pulled ahead, with the others a short distance behind. Clearing some trees, Leggert scanned the graying buildings for any sign of movement, then as he closed to within a hundred yards, a lone gunman stepped into the open.

"Far enough! Just ride off slow and easy!" the gunman shouted.

Leggert cupped his hands around his mouth

and shouted, "It's powerful wet out there. And we've ridden a far piece. We'd ride out but there ain't no shelter for at least thirty miles. Anyway, we're peaceable men."

Another outlaw appeared to confer with the one who'd challenged the deputies, and now he motioned them to ride on in. And they did so at a cautious walk. They rode past the outbuildings and into a compound and up to the outlaws. Only now, to the surprise of deputies Madden and Goddard, Dutch Leggert swung his horse around and jeered, "Arlo, Ray, want you to meet Bo Layden and Cal Widen."

"What the—"

"Go for it, Ray." Leggert grinned.

"You're in with these outlaws?"

"For a spell now. Best open them slickers and pass over your sidearms, and rifles."

"We ain't got no choice," said Arlo Goddard, "under the circumstances. Just what are your plans for us, Leggert?"

Gunrunner Bo Layden spat out, "You probably won't leave here alive, gents. That'll be determined when the bossman shows up. Your weapons!"

In his early thirties, Arlo Goddard knew he could either make a break for it or surrender his weapons. But what rang true about what the outlaw had just said was that Goddard knew this was it for him. What he couldn't stomach, or forgive, was the way Dutch Leggert had suckered them in. He returned Leggert's grin and shrugged.

"No sense arguing about it. Mind if I get down first?"

Cal Widen said, "Yeah, then we can get out of this rain."

Throwing a leg over the cantle, Goddard began easing out of the saddle, and when his right leg touched the ground, he punched his horse in the flank and it leaped forward and at the gunrunners as Goddard drew his .38 rimfire. As one of the gunrunners recovered and pumped a shot at him, Goddard leveled on Dutch Leggert, pumping shells into the man's chest and midriff. Then Arlo Goddard staggered, tried to swing his handgun on the others, only to be struck in the chest, and he came unlimbered and began falling. Vaguely, and just before a deep blackness overcame him, Goddard heard the frantic cries of Ray Madden from where he still sat in the saddle, the volley of gunfire, and somehow it seemed the other deputy was dropping out of the saddle.

The sudden outburst of gunfire brought the rest of the gunrunners out of the buildings and closing in on the compound. The outlaw in charge, Ed Rayburn, exclaimed, "What the hell, that's Leggert!"

"Dead—same's that one."

"Water," gasped Ray Madden, "please . . . water . . ."

Rayburn gazed down at the wounded deputy and said, "He's another deputy out of Arcadia. How did this happen, Bo?"

"That one tried to get away. Shot Leggert."

"I'll bet," snarled Rayburn. "Maybe you started it. And just maybe there's some soldiers out there. Get him some water. I want to find out what's up."

Untying the canteen from Madden's saddle horn, a gunrunner knelt down, cradled Madden's head in his arm, and said, "Here's some water. Easy, now. What about it—was it just the three of you?"

"Yeah . . . just us . . ." He clutched at the outlaw's shirt.

"You ain't lying about this?"

"They're coming . . . too . . ."

"More soldiers?"

The wounded deputy stiffened and gasped in pain, and then he smiled and muttered weakly, "soldiers . . . more soldiers . . ." Ray Madden knew that he was dying, that the last thing he could do was to protect the marshal of Arcadia and those riding with him, and somehow he summoned up a bitter laugh. "They're coming . . ."

"Damn you!" Ed Rayburn muttered. Pulling out his handgun, he grabbed Madden by the hair and pulled him to a sitting position and thrust the gun barrel into Madden's mouth. "Say you're lying, damn you!" But the eyes staring into his were glazing, and, angered that Dutch Leggert had been killed and at his own uncertainties, Ed pulled the trigger and blew the back of Ray Madden's head away. He stepped away from the body and glared at his men.

"A hell of a mess! Paragon and the others ain't here yet!" He shoved the gun back into its holster. "And some soldiers might be riding in any moment."

"It'll take some time to throw those packs on the horses and vamoose out of here, Ed. Besides, we got cover and they don't."

"Yeah, Bo, you're right. No sense doing something stupid. But I want some men to saddle up and follow their tracks back up along the river. And, Bo, check out their saddlebags and see if there's any whiskey. The rest of you, scatter out among the buildings and be ready just in case we get company."

CHAPTER NINETEEN

From the front balcony of the Regent Hotel the somber eyes of Laurel Jericho went to still another stagecoach arriving at White Sulphur Springs. The sprawling town had grown up around sulphur springs with the same mineral content as the famed waters at Baden Baden, Germany. However, Laurel's thoughts were on a town farther north in territorial Montana—Arcadia. There had only been the one letter from her son, Brad, in which he told of being appointed town marshal, a briefer mention of some rancher's daughter. As for Laurel, she had come here at the insistent of cattle baron Sam Waterman.

The long-sleeved dress showed to advantage Laurel's full figure. It was her own creation, dark blue with lacy ruffles. She'd also made the hat pinned to her upswept hair. Back in Bozeman Laurel had opened a millinery shop—a modest venture that gave her a comfortable living. There had been many towns before this, places she barely remembered, though Denver would always remain a part of her. For this was where she had given birth to her son. For a while she had considered taking her maiden name again, but a boy needed his father's name. It was here that a letter had caught up with Laurel telling her of an inheritance. Five thousand wasn't a princely sum, but it had given her outright ownership of the millinery shop.

Among those who'd come courting was Sam Waterman, a widower in his early sixties, whose gruff manners and rugged appearance concealed a kind heart. The trouble was that Laurel didn't love the rancher, nor could she explain to Sam that she'd never divorced her husband, Lane. Perhaps he was dead by now. Though he very well could be, somehow Laurel had the feeling the man she'd married and ran out on was still alive. Only to herself would Laurel admit that she was still in love with Lane, hoping that by leaving him he would come to his senses and give up his gambling, gunfighting life. She had sent one telegram, received no reply. And so the months and years had slipped by, leaving Laurel with a son to raise along with a vain attempt at healing her sorrowing heart.

Here at the Regent they were lodged in separate rooms, Sam to partake of the medicinal springs, and Laurel to attempt to enjoy herself in this aura of opulence and wealth.

Now the stagecoach swung around a corner and came down the bustling street to draw up across from the hotel. A lot of carriages and horsemen were passing by, too, and about the town was a spirit of prosperity. Along with the older buildings newer ones were springing up, while an editorial in the local newspaper told of the Northern Pacific considering putting in a spur line.

"Pardon me, but isn't that a gorgeous view?" she heard a woman say.

Laurel turned away from the railing and smiled back at an older woman. "I wonder what they call those mountains?"

"They're the Big Belts. I'm Clara Baldwin."

"Laurel Jericho—from Bozeman."

"Pretty name. I see you're with Sam Waterman."

"Oh, you know Sam?"

"Being the wife of a rancher I do. Sam's a fine man. Sort of let go after his wife passed away. He seems serious about you."

Laurel felt herself blush. She strolled with Clara Baldwin along the balcony and, at her invitation, went into the dining room for coffee and sweet rolls. A waitress brought them over to a table by one of the front windows. Laurel caught a glimpse of high-heeled boots under the long black skirt as Clara Baldwin settled down across from her. A flowery clasp was pinned to Clara's white blouse, over which she had on a tan leather coat. Unlike Laurel with her long tapering fingers and quiet sensual beauty, the ranchwoman was a handsome woman with a sunburned face and ample figure. Afternoon sunlight slanted through the windowpanes onto the white tablecloth as the waitress came back with their order.

"As I said, Laurel, Sam's a fine man."

"That he is. Perhaps . . ."

"Don't worry," laughed Clara, "I've seen that look in his eye." Then she glanced out through the window at several horsemen riding in to tie up across the street, and anger narrowed her eyes. "Well I'll be . . . Bo Layden has got his gall showing up in these parts again. Worked for us for a spell. Then he stole some of our horses and vamoosed."

Out in the street, Jay Paragon gathered the nine men close and said, "I don't want any of you gettin' in trouble. You know why we're here."

Snarled Bo Layden, "To kill them lawmen in case they show up."

The long ride down into the South River valley had been uneventful until they arrived at Camp Baker just after the weather had started to clear. There they saw some of the men clustered around the new mounds of dirt just west of the buildings, and he rode over and was told by Ed Rayburn that one of the dead men was Dutch Leggert.

"Expecting some soldiers to show up most anytime, Jay."

"We came across only three sets of tracks."

"Dammit, one of them deputies swore some soldiers were out there."

"And you swallowed that lie."

"Wasn't taking no chances."

"Which makes me wonder," pondered Paragon, "just who sent those deputies down here. Got to be the marshal of Arcadia. I figure when we left Bennett's place, these deputies followed your bunch, Ed, with Marshal Brad Jericho picking up our trail over to Cadotte Pass."

"How'd it go?"

"Like we planned. Right about now Mackley's halfway to Miles City. But the question is, did Marshal Jericho go after Mackley or follow us down here?"

"Probably got a posse with him."

"Yeah. You're probably fixed for grub same as us. Which means we're moving out."

"About time. Where we headed, Big Timber?"

"Don't want to get there too early. So, Ed, we'll get the horses ready and make camp down by White Sulphur Springs. We'll take turns watching those packhorses."

"I hear that place is a going town."

"The last thing I want is trouble down there." He walked his horse alongside Ed Bradley as others moved closer. "I've a hunch that marshal picked up our trail and is after us. If so, he'll tail us to White Sulphur Springs. Which is where we're gonna punch his lights out."

"You think that U.S. marshal and the mountie are with him?"

"Better for us if they are."

"It'll save us a lot of worry if they come here."

Jay Paragon nodded downstreet. "Their first order of business will be to send a telegram. Bo, keep an eye on that telegraph office."

The hardcase grumbled, "Have someone else do it. I'm craving some whiskey."

"Just do it," snapped Paragon. "I'll relieve you in an hour."

Major Dirk Mackley brought his detachment of gunrunners cantering along Great Porcupine Creek lowering onto the Yellowstone River flood plain. It had taken them almost a week to get here, with both Mackley and Sgt. Flin Colmar trying to make cavalrymen out of this riffraff. Mackley's upraised arm halted the column on the north bank of the Yellowstone. He reached into a saddlebag for his field glass as Sergeant Colmar rode along the raggedy column and inspected his troops.

"You know that train'll be pulling in late this afternoon. You've been briefed on what to expect . . . what you're going to do."

"Hey, Sarge, what's that word 'briefed' mean?"

Colmar forced a smile. "It means you're to act and think like soldiers. According to what the major told me, there'll be cattle cars for our horses. So for now we'll make camp under those trees."

"I knew I should'a went with Paragon. Had my fill of the army back in '78. Now I gotta wear me a uniform again."

"You desert, Shipley?"

"What the hell else!"

"All right, listen up. I know you'd like to head in and slake your thirst at the saloons. The major's going in first to scout the place out. Then he'll fetch back some grub . . . and some whiskey." Colmar swung his horse around and rode back to Mackley just lowering the field glass.

"I can see a section of track but not the depot. I suspect, Flin, that troops from nearby Fort Keogh are standing by to see that the supply train passes through safely. While I'm in town, I'll announce my presence to whoever's in charge."

"Those orders you forged look awful convincing, sir."

"Should be, since they're the genuine article.

202

My only worry is that Marshal Tillison has sent a telegram down here."

"He couldn't have from Arcadia."

"Perhaps. What about them?"

"Still don't trust any of those gunrunners. But they're shaped up some. When we take them in, I suggest we get them aboard that train as quickly as possible."

"What I was thinking, Flin. It's drawing onto noon. Just thinking, too, that it would look out of character my coming in alone. But you'll have to stay here. What about that man wearing the corporal's uniform?"

"Shipley's a loud mouth, sir, but he's had some service time."

"He'll do."

Through a frown Colmar barked, "Get yourself over here, Shipley. You'll be going with the major into town."

The hardcase rode up and grinned. "I'm ready, sir."

Sgt. Flin Colmar waited until Mackley and Corporal Shipley had forded the sluggish waters of the Yellowstone before he brought his men under the concealing trees, where they tended to their horses. It would be a dry camp, he told them. Ever since leaving Cadotte Pass some six days ago, the fear of Flin Colmar had been that of being killed by Mackley. By rights he should have made a break for it. If he had, he would have been someplace in the Rockies by now and maybe clearing them on his way to the Oregon Territory. But that would have meant leaving Hannah behind. The bottom line, he realized, was that a woman and his own greed had led him into this trap. Any officer worth his salt would size up the mannerisms of these gunrunners and realize they weren't soldiers.

"Fretting about it ain't helping your ulcer none," Colmar muttered. "For if anyone can pull this off, Mackley can."

It wasn't Dirk Mackley's way to take a backstreet or road when coming into a town. So it was that after Mackley and his escort had crossed the river and found a road, they cantered along it and at Mackley's command swung their horses onto Main Street. Historically the street was a fragment of the trail between Fort Keogh and Bismarck. For when Miles City, or Milestown as it was originally called, sprang up it was to have the business section grow on either side of the road along which passed freighting trains, stages, and assorted travelers going to or from Bismarck, Bozeman, Fort Buford, Deadwood and various points in between. Miles City was also the county seat of Big Horn County embracing a section of southwestern Montana Territory equal in size to the state of Pennsylvania.

Having passed through here before, Major Mackley knew the train depot lay to the south of Main Street, along which he arrogantly rode.

"Well, Shipley, how does it feel to serve your country again?"

"If the goldang pay hadn't of been so puny, this old hoss would still be a-wearin' the blue, sir."

"Which is why I'm talking to you at the moment."

"Sure a lot of saloons . . ."

"First we'll dispose of the business at hand, Corporal."

Mackley followed the wide-spanned street curling to the west and when they passed a large wooden warehouse, he veered toward the railroad right of way, along which stood a siding, water tower, and the depot. The absence of soldiers told Mackley he was either early in getting here or the special train had been delayed. Drawing up by the depot, he let Shipley tend to their horses. He pulled off one glove while stepping up onto the platform, then returned the courteous nod of a baggage handler as he opened the office door and stepped inside. The unexpected presence of an old army acquaintance gave him pause.

"Dirk? Good to see you again."

Mackley peeled off the other glove and extended his hand. "Anyone deserves to be light colonel, it's you, Phil."

"Heard you were stationed out at Fort Shaw. What brings you here?"

"Orders." Mackley pulled out the folded sheet of paper and passed it to Col. Phil Travers. "Thought I'd come in early and get a hand on the situation, but it still seems a waste of time escorting a supply train through these parts."

"You haven't heard about these gunrunners?"

"Heard plenty about them. Look, Phil, we have forts strung along the Northern Pacific right of way . . . a lot of other places in Montana. If these gunrunners are as smart as we think they are, for certain they'll know better than to attack this train."

"I'm here on orders from headquarters. Seems you are too. How many men did you bring along?"

"Just a patrol, Phil. Thought we'd board the train here; tag along until it gets to Bozeman. Where I'm told others will take over."

"We can use you, Dirk. These gunrunners have to be stopped. So far they've killed at least ten soldiers. Anyway, the train's scheduled to pull in at 3:10."

He smiled back at Colonel Travers. "Which could also mean 3:10 in the morning. It's damned tough keeping schedules out here. But we'll be here and ready to go. Damn, Phil, we went through a lot together. See you later." He threw the colonel a casual salute and let himself out.

With the sound of Mackley's horse clopping away filtering through an open window, Colonel Travers rose from behind the desk as the door running into a back corridor swung open. He gestured toward the desk. "Thanks for letting me use your office."

Wadsworth, the depot agent, said, "The Northern Pacific is always glad to help out when we can. I expect you'll be wanting to talk to Marshal Tillison in private. Coffee time for me anyway." The agent removed his coat and hat from a wall hook and brushed past Con Tillison as he left.

"You were right about Mackley showing up here."

The gunshot wound had thinned out Con Tillison. And his movements were that of a man savoring his strength, but his hands were steady when Tillison rolled a cigarette into shape. "I knew this some time back. Only I got bushwhacked on the way up to Fort Shaw."

"This man who is impersonating you — Jericho — do you think he's still alive?"

"For all intents and purposes Colonel De Trobriand is still under the impression those wires I've been sending came from Jericho. According to De Trobriand, Jericho and Sgt. Shawn Mac-Iver left for Arcadia several days ago. So did

Major Mackley."

"You still believe that Dirk Mackley went there to meet with Jay Paragon?"

"No question about it, Colonel. Nor is there any question about them knowing about this arms shipment."

Colonel Travers said, "An officer going bad. You know, Marshal, when Mackley came in, I had a hard time controlling my temper."

"You won't have to live with him much longer. Now, you're agreed, Colonel Travers, that nothing must happen here at Miles City. We'll let Mackley and those with him board the train. The question now is, just how much does Mackley know about where the train'll stop to take on coal and water. Perhaps he knows the entire operation. So, as you suggested, we'll stop the train just before we get to Billings."

"Soldiers from Fort Benton will be waiting. Then we can confront Mackley and make him tell us where the other gunrunners are." There was a rap at the door, and Travers went over and swung it open. "Sergeant Macon?"

"Sir, around fifteen soldiers are camped by the river."

"Get close enough to see if they're the real McCoy—"

"Got close enough, sir, to really glass them in. Some of the uniforms they're wearing are spouting bullet holes."

"Mackley'll answer for that too," the colonel said grimly.

"What about Mackley?" Con asked.

"Marshal, he's downtown buying supplies — but mostly whiskey."

"Which is where I'm going to chow down," said Tillison. "Don't worry, Colonel Travers, Dirk Mackley and I have never gotten acquainted. Something that's going to change mighty soon."

CHAPTER TWENTY

"No sense following those packhorses any longer."

"I agree with you," said Sgt. Shawn MacIver. "Paragon's the one we want. Should be in White Sulphur Springs right about now."

The two men, along with Brad Jericho, were sitting their horses where the tracks they'd been following had forked, the smaller bunch of gunrunners taking off toward White Sulphur Springs marked in the distance by palish light dusting the night sky. Westward, ambered moonlight revealed the Rockies' white-capped peaks. Behind them lay three unmarked graves, a sobering fact that drew them closer, making even Brad Jericho realize the need for caution from here on in.

"Their only reason for calling at that town," said MacIver, "is to stock up on supplies. Could be, too, that Mackley sent a telegram to tell Paragon if everything's all right."

Lane Jericho spoke up. "There's the possibility

one of your deputies spilled the beans about us coming after Paragon. Which means Paragon could be setting a trap for us at that town."

"We'll have to chance it," said MacIver as he rode on with the others. "Because it's imperative we send a wire to inform the army about those gunrunners."

After a while the southwesterly moon showed them a road, which, Lane figured, ran from Camp Logan to White Sulphur Springs barely a mile to the south. Lane wasn't overly superstitious, nor was he prone to fret over things, but in him was this sense of expectancy that his past was about to catch up with him. No, it couldn't be, and he dislodged from his mind the strange notion that Laurel would be here. With those gunrunners awaiting them, this was no time to set his thoughts on the wife he'd lost so many years ago. As the road flowed up a dusty ridge and they crested it, Lane got a good look at the town throwing out light and noise. The road bunched in between outlying buildings, and farther on, Lane eyed with some bemusement a white steepled church. Beyond that a couple of brick houses, and at their approach a yellow dog bounded out from behind a hedgerow and began baying.

"At least that dog knows we're here," said Lane.

"This town has the look of prosperity."

"Paid for by those coming here," Brad told them, "to use the medicinal waters. You'll find no dance halls or gambling joints. Just the usual run of saloons."

"It's getting late," MacIver said as a high-sided wagon turned the corner and headed their way, and with his wave caused the teamster to rein up. "Sorry to trouble you, mister, but we're looking for the telegraph office."

"Back there on the main drag. It's still open, but I'd hurry."

"What about the marshal's office?"

"A block farther down."

Riding on, they turned onto a wide street angling to the east and past large hotels, shops, or mercantile stores and saloons. Tethered along the street were a few horses. A big-wheeled carriage passing by drew their attention to it as did the curried bay in the traces. Lane glanced at MacIver.

"No sense all of us going along to send that wire." Lane said. "That hotel yonder looks inviting. Me and Brad here can get us some rooms."

"I want one with a view," said MacIver. "Yes, there's the Wells Fargo office. Should have an operator on duty."

"Be careful you don't run into those renegades."

"Never had the pleasure of meeting any of them," MacIver said. "After I get through doing this chore, we can find a livery stable."

"Seems to be one up that side street," said Brad, and MacIver nodded as he rode away. Then Brad followed Lane over to a hitching rail, where they dismounted. "Why don't you sign the register while I take care of our horses."

"Obliged," smiled Lane.

The solarium attached to the back wall of the Regent Hotel was of circular construction and some sixty feet in radius. It opened on the sulphur spring baths, provided a lounge by day and at night a gathering place for entertainment. People strolled about or sat on the chaise lounges, and moonlight reflected through the big encircling windows. Tonight's entertainers were a pianist and soprano going through a medley of operatic songs. And wanting to leave were ranchers Baldwin and Waterman. To further emphasize his displeasure at being here, E.T. Baldwin relit his cigar.

He remarked testily, "Clara, this is no place for one used to the ways of the wild."

"A little culture, E.T., is just what you need."

"He's right, Clara," said Sam Waterman with a sideways smile for Laurel Jericho. "Perhaps a little stroll will give us a nice dose of clear air and a chance to be heard."

"Got to admit she's an awful loud singer. What

do you say, Laurel? After all it was Sam who dragged us here."

"Yes, I'd like some fresh air."

"Now you're talking, ladies."

They passed into the lobby and crossed to the main entrance, and as Sam Waterman opened the door, he said quietly while patting his coat pocket, "Been meaning to show you this before, Laurel. Just haven't dug up the courage to do so until tonight. It's—it's . . . well, why don't we find us a place that serves drinks and I'll get it over with?"

"Why, Sam, I do believe you're blushing."

"Now, Clara, don't be a-picking on Sam. But a drink will sure enough ease this parched throat of mine."

Out on the street, Laurel Jericho knew from the way Sam had just acted that he was about to propose marriage. She forced a smile for Waterman and the others as they came to an intersection and paused to let some cowhands lope by. She scanned their faces, hoping that one of them would be her son. As she stepped out into the street with the others, Laurel chanced to gaze up-street at the Western Hotel located in the middle of the block. There was something familiar about the man who'd just emerged from its main entrance, but his back was to her. Then a large man came out followed by Brad Jericho. She pulled up short and tugged at Waterman's arm.

214

"I believe that's my son. Coming out of that hotel."

"You mean Brad?"

"Yes. It is—" Laurel choked off the rest of what she had been about to say, for her face had suddenly gone ashy when she recognized Lane Jericho striding between the other two men. "My God . . . Lane?" She swayed and would have fallen had not Sam Waterman steadied her. Now a scream tore from Laurel's throat when the night exploded.

Upon entering the Wells Fargo office tucked in between a hardware store and a storage building, Shawn MacIver moved away from the door and peered through a front window at the bustling street. Either he was being followed or someone was keeping an eye on this place. He felt this as well as he knew the workings of his rifle. Which meant to MacIver that the gunrunners were still hanging around town.

"That sign says no loafing, mister."

Swinging around, he strode up to the counter and revealed to the clerk on duty his identification, and said softly, "Has anybody been in here asking whether or not some lawmen have showed up?"

"Not since I came on duty. But while going for coffee I spotted some hardcases idling just up the street."

"That telegraph set in working order?"

"Line's up, if that's what you mean."

MacIver reached for a blank pad and a pencil stub and began scribbling out a message. "Keep sending this message until you get a response from the military over at Miles City."

"At Miles City?"

"Correct, sir. Then send the same message to Bozeman." Handing the pad to the clerk, he pulled out some paper money and slapped it down on the counter. "Now, try that machine and see if it's still working."

The clerk went and sat down before the telegraph set and began working the key. "Line's still working."

"Keep at it until it goes dead."

"Cutting the line is a criminal offense, sir."

"So's spitting on the street." Stepping back to a front window, MacIver studied those he saw standing about or moving past the building. He felt uneasy, knowing that before coming here he should have checked in with the town marshal and explained the situation. If anything happened tonight, it would be just the three of them against at least a dozen gunrunners. And there was every possibility they could be taken out. Exiting onto the street, MacIver rode his horse over to the livery stable, then made his way over to the hotel to find Lane Jericho waiting for him in the lobby.

"How'd it go?"

"Got that message sent. Where's Brad?"

"Upstairs getting acquainted with some soap and water."

"They might have had someone watching that telegraph office. If so, now they know we're in town. After we wash away this trail grit, Lane, I suggest we find the local marshal."

At a nearby corner downstreet from the hotel, Bo Layden swung away and went to find Jay Paragon. He'd been keeping an eye on the Wells Fargo office when the mountie had gone in, and when MacIver left, he'd followed him here. He didn't know how many others had ridden in with Shawn MacIver, but it didn't matter, for in a little while all of them would be plugged full of leaden slugs. A couple of blocks to the east the hardcase shoved through batwings and looked around before spotting Paragon seated at a poker table, and he sauntered over.

"They're here, Jay. Like you said, they went over to the telegraph office. Trailed 'em back to the Western Hotel."

Wordlessly, Paragon threw down his cards and picked up his chips as he shoved away from the table. He brought Bo Layden back to where some of his men were clustered around a pool table. "Those lawmen just rode in. Where's Driscoll, the Rayburn brothers, the others?"

217

"Out hunting up some fun, I reckon."

"Those shiftless no-goods," Paragon muttered angrily. "I want this thing with those lawmen settled tonight. We've got what supplies we need stowed in our saddlebags—enough to see us to Big Timber and beyond, if that becomes necessary. All right, five of us can handle this. First we'll make sure our horses are saddled and then—"

"Damn, Jay, those hotel rooms looked awful comfortable."

"There'll be plenty of time for easy livin' after this job is over. After we get them weapons up to the métis. Is that clear?"

"You're the bossman."

The hardcases hurried out the back door and over to a nearby livery stable, where they saddled their horses, and at Paragon's insistence, the mounts of the missing hardcases. "Once we open up on Jericho and those other lawmen, our bunch'll come running. Anyway, they know where to find the packhorses. Time's a-wasting." An impatient Jay Paragon led his men out of the livery stable and toward the Western Hotel.

Lane Jericho rapped on the door before entering MacIver's hotel room. A moment later Brad Jericho arrived, and Lane said, "We'll have to tread softly tonight since Paragon must know we're here."

"Supper can wait until we talk to the town marshal. I'm sure he can muster up a few men once we explain the urgency of the situation." Shawn MacIver buckled on his gun belt. "Down here neither my badge nor yours, Brad, carries any weight."

"All I want is Jay Paragon, the dirty killer."

"There's more than Paragon out there," cut in Lane. "A man of his caliber's got to be awful good with a gun—as are those riding for him. With them it's kill now and to hell with the right or wrong of it. I just don't want you to let your anger cloud your judgment."

"You're not my father," jeered Brad Jericho. "All I know is I'm a lawman same's you. And probably a better man with a gun."

"Okay," said MacIver, "for now let's try to get along. And just maybe if Marshal Tillison was your father, lad, he'd sting your backside a few times. What I'm saying, Marshal Brad Jericho, is that we're in charge of this now. True, we need your gun. But if you think otherwise about this, now's the time to back out."

Scowling at Lane, and then at MacIver, Brad said tautly, "Maybe I spouted off some. Maybe them killing Mr. Bennett, my deputies, is more than I can handle at the moment. But I'll just have to push that aside. Okay, count me in."

"You have any words for him?"

Lane eyed the mountie and said, "Not the words you want me to say right now. And if apologies are needed, I'll say them later." He went out first, trying to fight down the concern he had for his son. That explosive temper of Brad's needed to have its fuse tamped. The set to Lane's face caused the man he'd just passed in the corridor to take a backward glance, then Lane was going down the staircase and giving the lobby a careful look, with Brad trailing MacIver. Lane stepped to the desk and inquired as to whether the town marshal was on duty tonight.

"Mostly he is. But otherwise he's over at Birdy's Saloon."

Nodding, Lane went over and moving outside, held the door open for the others. As he stood there, he studied those moving past on the boardwalk, swung his eyes to the opposite side of the street to find that most of the business places had shut down for the night. He knew something was wrong. There'd been too many other places like this, of his being sought by gunmen, and he spoke softly to MacIver, "They're out there waiting for us."

"I know." He fell into step with Lane as Brad Jericho moved up on the inside. "The jail's a block past the telegraph office. That is, if they let us get that far."

"Worried?" Lane smiled.

"Worry comes with the job."

Lane felt a little better when they stepped under a wooden porch but just ahead of them was a street lamp, and before that the yawning black mouth of an alleyway. He brushed the tail of his coat away from his Smith & Wesson, some sixth sense telling him that once they cleared this porch the gunrunners would open up. Now a great anguish tore at Lane Jericho. Here he'd found his son, only the boy didn't know it, and in a few seconds either Brad or maybe all three of them would be dead. He couldn't have that happen.

"Thought I saw something on that roof across the street," MacIver remarked quietly.

"You probably did," responded Lane, and then as they cleared the porch and closed on the alley, the gunrunners opened up. Lane's gun cleared leather, but instead of firing back at the ambushers, he clubbed the barrel across the back of Brad's head, caught him as he was falling and dragged his son into the alley. Then MacIver was at Lane's side between the buildings and firing back at blued muzzle flashes. A slug tore into Lane and he grunted in surprise, with his Smith & Wesson driving a gunrunner back to have the man crumble through a store window.

MacIver, who'd set his back against a wall, began reloading his empty weapon, and he said, "I winged a couple."

"Sent one shopping for a new suit. They don't

seem awful anxious to close in."

"The way of coyotes." As the fire slackened off, MacIver triggered a volley of slugs at three men breaking away. One of them suddenly pitched forward on his face, but the men the hardcase was with never stopped to help one of their own.

"Seems they're cutting out," Lane said.

"Probably figure on riding out and hooking up with the others. So, where does that leave us?"

"Cutting out after them, Shawn."

"You're hit?"

"Nothing I can't live with."

"And, also Lane, that was a cute way of taking your son out of action."

"I owe his mother that much. Well, you ready to take off after them?"

"What about your son?"

"We'll leave the marshal of Arcadia behind to explain things to a fellow town marshal."

"Lane, you're one ornery cuss."

CHAPTER TWENTY-ONE

"He's coming around."

The upholder of the law in White Sulphur Springs, Milo Thurmond, put the coffeepot he'd just picked up back on the stove in his office and crossed to the cells strung along one wall.

"Still can't figure this gent packing a marshal's badge," said the deputy.

"What about it, mister," rasped Thurmond, "the minute you show up all hell busts loose."

Blinking his eyes open, Brad Jericho let the moment of dizziness pass before he swung his legs to the floor and pushed up from the cast-iron bunk. He grasped a cell bar to steady himself while placing a hand to the back of his head.

"Well, we're waiting?"

"Marshal, we chased some gunrunners down here."

"We?"

"Yeah, me . . . and a U.S. marshal and a

Canadian mountie—"

"That story sure cuts the mustard, mister."

"What I'm saying is gospel," said Brad. "I'm a marshal too—up at Arcadia."

"Been there. So your story don't hold water since I know who packs a lawman's badge up to Arcadia. Mister, you're facing a hanging offense."

"I'm telling you true about this." He blinked away another spasm of dizziness. "They've already killed a rancher up there and some of his men, and right about now they're heading south someplace."

"Let's start with your name?"

"Brad Jericho . . . marshal of Arcadia."

Milo Thurmond gestured toward Brad's star-pointed badge lying on his desk. "Outlaws have been known to pack them before. Another thing, Jericho, if that's your real name, your friends pulled out leaving you to answer for those killings."

"Look," Brad said desperately, "Sergeant MacIver sent a telegram shortly after we got here. It was to warn the army about these gunrunners coming their way. Check this out at the Wells Fargo office. What you should be doing now is forming a posse and taking after those gunrunners."

"Four in the morning ain't no time to roust out the citizenry. Come sun-up, I'll check out your story."

"You do that," Brad said, and to himself, "Yeah, you do that." He found the bunk again as the marshal turned out the coal-oil lantern and left with his deputy.

As he lay there, Brad Jericho felt that deep well of bitterness he had for Marshal Con Tillison spilling out of his squinting eyes. How could Tillison have suckered him like that, left him behind to answer for what had happened? After a while sleep overcame Brad.

Some time later, the sound of a door being opened and the voice of a woman woke him. He dropped the shielding arm away from his eyes to find his mother moving toward his cell.

"Brad . . . Oh, darling, I saw what happened."

"What are you doing here?" He stood up and hurried over to the bars of the cell to run a comforting hand cross her cheek.

"How bad is it?"

"Got hit over the head is all. Well, I can't believe you're here."

"I came over here with friends," said Laurel.

"And some friends I have," he blurted out. "They just up and left me here. That damnable Tillison . . . I want him bad . . .

"Tillison must be the big man," questioned Laurel.

"That'll be the mountie name of MacIver."

"You mean you don't know?"

"Just what am I supposed to know?"

"The other man is your father—Lane. Lane Jericho!"

"That . . . cant' be? He's . . . he's a U.S. marshal."

"He may be that too, Brad, but truly he's your father. How did he find you? And . . . and what's this all about?"

"I guess it's about being a lawman. Maybe of not doing my duty when I should have. Otherwise Julia's father would still be alive." He gazed past Laurel at the deputy shouldering into the jail.

"Like he said, Milo, someone claiming to be a Canadian mountie sent out a couple of telegrams last night. Shortly afterward, according to the Wells Fargo clerk, this wire arrived." He dropped it on the desk.

"Detachment commanded by Major Dirk Mackley," Thurmond read, "boarded Northern Pacific special train late yesterday afternoon. Military units plan to stop train at undisclosed point and arrest Mackley. Other units will head for Big Timber in order to intercept rest of gunrunners." He turned and stared at Brad Jericho. "This was sent by some army officer over at Miles City. Just maybe you are telling the truth."

"I've been doing that all along. Look, Marshall, I know this is army business, but those who came into town with me could be in trouble."

"Just what can I do?"

"Form a posse. Then let me ride with you to Big Timber."

"Gunrunners, you say?"

"That and all of them killers. I'll tell you about it on the way."

"That's good enough for me." Reaching for his ring of keys, the marshal unlocked Brad's cell while telling his deputy to head over and ring the church bell.

Putting on his hat, Brad came out of the cell and swept Laurel into his arms. He kissed her on the forehead as his eyes locked on hers. "Strange, Mom, but I knew I'd seen him before . . . Tillison."

"His picture's in that locket I gave you."

"Didn't even think about that. Why didn't he tell me?"

"Remembering how Lane was, maybe he was afraid to. It's been a lot of years. Your father must have been looking for us all this time. But how did he know about you?"

"I'll get the answer to that when we catch up with him and MacIver. Mom, I have to go. Where'll you be—still here or back at Bozeman?"

"Brad, I . . . I," said Laurel through misting eyes, "can't leave now. Come back to me. I'll stay on at the Regent Hotel."

"What about . . . Lane?"

"I suppose that's for him to decide."

"You still love him, don't you?"

"Always have, Brad Jericho. Suppose I always will."

Forcing a smile, he said, "I still owe him for whacking me on the side of the head . . . and some snide words. But just maybe . . . he did it to keep me from getting killed."

CHAPTER TWENTY-TWO

The engineer piloting Northern Pacific locomotive 553 sat before his controls in his spacious cab while gazing out a side window at the undulating plains of Montana. Every so often the fireman would toss chunks of wood into the boiler while joshing with the soldier assigned to guard them in case the gunrunners attacked the train. Back at Miles City those soldiers who'd stabled their horses in the cattle car seemed to be a shabby lot, a feeling shared by the engineer and the others.

Pulling out his big turnip-shaped watch, engineer Clinton said, "We're keeping to schedule. But I see no reason for Colonel Travers wanting me to stop just this side of Billings."

"That's the army."

"Amen for the railroad at times."

"That moon helps some. Remember the times we couldn't travel at night because of the buffalo. Thousands of them critters."

In the only club car assigned to the train, that coupled ahead of the passenger cars carrying soldiers, a handful of officers including Major Dirk Mackley were being briefed by Colonel Travers. That group included Marshal Con Tillison sipping brandy from a glass. While just in front of the club car were the cars bearing military arms being shipped to Western outposts.

"That's it, gentlemen, what we'll do in case those gunrunners try something. Much to our good fortune Major Mackley brought along some more troops."

"I have it on good authority," said Tillison, "that soldiers could be involved in this."

"Entirely possible," Travers replied. "Every so often you hear about some soldier or even officer getting mixed up in something. Ours isn't a perfect army, Marshal."

Tillison laughed softly. "No question but that there've been a few crooked lawmen too." He'd said that for Mackley's benefit, who sat across from him but closer to the rear of the club car and in another padded chair. They were closing on Billings, he knew, and he would be glad when this was over so that he could put in for leave and get away for a while. The problem of Lane Jericho posing as Tillison had been solved by Colonel Travers' introducing him as a Mr. Charles Willard, a representative of the War Department, and now Tillison looked at Dirk

Mackley.

"Tell me, Major, do you think these gunrunners will show?"

"Sir, your guess is as good as mine. This whole incident has given the army a bad name, I'm afraid. You've even got me thinking that some of my men at Fort Shaw could be involved in this."

"Perhaps," murmured Tillison, savoring what was to come, for only he and Colonel Travers knew that in a few minutes locomotive 553 would be coasting to a stop. In anticipation of this he pushed his glass aside and shifted his weight on the chair so that his coat was free of his holstered sidearm. Briefly, he caught Travers' eye and cast an impulsive wink at it, which caused the colonel to stroke his mustache to hide the sudden smile.

Then Colonel Travers commented that they seemed to be slowing down and, along with the others, turned and gazed out of the side windows to discover what had caused this unexpected change in speed. Only Con Tillison's eyes went to Mackley as he unlimbered his handgun.

"Why are we stopping?"

"Got no idea why, Dirk," said another officer, a captain.

The screeching of metal on metal came to them as the train lost momentum, then one of the officers exclaimed, "There seems to be cav-

231

alry strung along that bluff."

"More on this side."

"Colonel, any idea what's up?"

"I do, Mackley. Consider yourself under arrest!"

"What? How dare you?"

"Easy," said Tillison as Dirk Mackley's hand dropped to his holstered weapon. "You'll live a while longer that way."

"Who are you?"

"A U.S. marshal name of Con Tillison."

"Sir, this man's an imposter," Mackley said. "Marshal Tillison is at Fort Shaw right now."

"Mackley, damn you, the game's over. Do as the marshal says, hand over your sidearm." Colonel Travers steadied himself as the train lurched to a stop on a railroad trestle hanging over a dark-enshrouded river.

His face bleached and hatred pouring out of his eyes, Dirk Mackley unbuckled his belt, and before anyone could anticipate his intention, he flung his holstered weapon at a nearby lantern and at the same time broke for the door. In the uncertain light Tillison fired wildly, then Mackley was gone.

Pulling a hideout gun out of his coat pocket, a frightened Dirk Mackley rushed through a passenger car, entered a second occupied by the gunrunners and Sgt. Flin Colmar.

Colmar yelled, "What's wrong, Mackley?" Now

he rose to block the aisle.

Mackley kept on coming as he pulled the trigger again, managed to get past Flin Colmar's body crumbling to the floor. He came out of the car and onto the vestibule and lunged down onto the trestle. He had to get away, but where, since to both sides horsemen were moving in. Now the glinting river caught his eye. He made his way to the wooden support girders and without hesitating let himself go. He struck cold water and went under, with the twisting currents sweeping him downriver and away from the train.

Aboard the train, the gunrunners broke the windows with their weapons and began firing at the horsemen swinging down off their mounts and forming skirmish lines.

"We ain't got no chance against that many soldiers!" one of the hardcases, Shipley, cried out.

"It's either fighting back or surrendering and being taken someplace to get hanged."

"I'll take my chances in court any day," Shipley said. "You men better make up your minds before they get the command to fire back."

"Shipley's right! Those repeating rifles will slice right through this passenger car. Well, dammit, I'm calling it quits!"

After the gunrunners had surrendered, the search for Dirk Mackley brought soldiers scouting both sides of the river, while the supply train resumed its westward trek. Part of the plan laid out by Tillison was to question the gunrunners, and one by one they were brought into the club car.

"Your name?"

"Shipley."

Tillison grimaced. "You kill that soldier to get his uniform?"

"I was in on it," Shipley admitted.

"You're the first of your breed to admit anything. We want Jay Paragon."

"Expect as much. How's about cutting a deal, Marshal?"

"Go on—"

"Like I get sentenced to prison instead of dancing at the end of a rope."

"Shipley, that could be worked out."

"It'll happen when you get to Big Timber."

Colonel Travers said, "How many men does Paragon have?"

"Twenty-five or so, I reckon."

"For once," said Tillison, "the odds are on our side. By the way, Shipley, were you one of those who ambushed me?"

"Nossir. Tom Driscoll bragged about taking you out. Driscoll will be one of those waiting at Big Timber."

"By the way, Shipley, the military has the authority out here."

"What's that supposed to mean?"

"It means I have no power to strike a deal

with scum like you."

The hardcase tried to lunge at Tillison but was held back by the restraining hands of two soldiers. "Damn you, Marshal, we made a deal. I sure as sin don't wanna hang. Don't deserve to after telling you about what's gonna happen at Big Timber."

"And the soldier whose uniform you're wearing didn't deserve what he got! Take him away."

CHAPTER TWENTY-THREE

For the better part of the day Jay Paragon's gunrunners had skirted the western flanks of the Rockies. Then in the fading hours of daylight they veered southwesterly toward the lesser Crazies gnawing its bony peaks at the darkening sky. It would be after midnight when they reached Big Timber on the Yellowstone River.

Anger still gripped Jay Paragon over their not taking out those lawmen back at White Sulphur Springs, a big share of it because they could have done the job had his other men been there. As a result, two of his men were dead. Later there'd be a score to settle with the Rayburn brothers, the others.

The packhorses were strung out in a long line. Shadows were stealing away from the mountains to the east when one of the point riders came back to tell them of a creek in their line of travel. Upon coming to the creek, Paragon ordered a halt, then barely gave his men and the

236

horses a chance to water up before he brought them on the move again.

"Jay, we don't have to be there until morning."

"It's not where we're going that's eating at my craw, Driscoll. Those lawmen are back there."

"There was only three of them."

"They could have gotten a posse together." As the wind picked up, Paragon tugged down his hat. "So we get to Big Timber only to find out Mackley got himself into trouble along the way. Meaning he don't show. There's no way we can tackle that train by ourselves."

"There'll always be another supply train."

"But not people like those métis needing guns and ammo, Driscoll. I just don't like the way things are going."

"It'll work out, Jay, it always has before." He broke into a pleased whistle.

"How you holding out, Lane?"

"Just a flesh wound."

"It hit deeper than that," said MacIver. "Or it could just be you're tough-skinned as well as hard of heart. You should have told your son who you are."

"At least he's still alive."

"That's a fact," smiled the mountie.

They were past the Crazies now and by moonlight were picking up occasional glimpses of the tracks left by the gunrunners. Ahead of them, they knew, lay the Yellowstone River, and some place along it the Northern Pacific line passing through Big Timber. Their only hope of stopping Jay Paragon was that the telegrams MacIver had sent from White Sulphur Springs had gotten into the right hands.

MacIver gestured toward a row of trees and said tiredly, "Let's pull up over there. Take a breather."

"I could sure use one." Among the trees, Lane slid down from his horse and moved after MacIver closing on a narrow stream. Hunkering down, Lane flexed the fingers of his left hand and grimaced at the twinge of pain coming from the shoulder wound. His probing fingers had determined that the slug had passed on through, and for now, a makeshift bandage would have to do the job. Then he soaked his bandanna in the cooling water and washed trail dust from his face. After that he felt a little better.

"Here, have some beef jerky."

"You know, back there at White Sulphur Springs, I had the craziest feeling that my wife was there. Guess aging does that to a man, makes his mind play all sorts of tricks."

"And if she had been?"

"Probably wouldn't have remembered me, or worse, taken after me with a Greener. Never know about women."

"I'll be gone to blazes, Jericho, you still love the woman." He laughed and gnawed a piece of jerky away with his teeth.

"I love, MacIver," he said after a while, "what we shared. A dream that got away from me. I don't know—just thinking about her saddens the hell out of me."

"At least you sired a fine son."

"One with a considerable temper. Guess we'd best ride on, Shawn. Just how much farther is it to this Big Timber town anyway?"

"Down yonder over them hills and such. They don't have that much of a head start on us, Lane."

They headed out again, and Lane murmured, "I don't want to catch them just to stampede their packhorses. That won't accomplish anything. Rest easy, Shawn, 'cause I know the army received your wires. They'll bring in a heap of soldiers to stop these killers."

Around four or so in the morning those chasing the gunrunners urged their horses on under a sky beginning to lighten. They had passed a few ranches battened down for the night, had stopped to water their horses at a water tank a few miles back as the moon passed beyond the Rockies, and so for a spell they'd lost the tracks they'd been following—only to pick them up when coming around a lonely butte. At the moment Lane couldn't be sure in the uncertain light if what he

239

saw to the south was the outline of a town above the fringing treeline. They angled that way as streaks of crimson pushed back more gray and a few more shadows slunk back into their holes. Now they were certain it was Big Timber when the labored chug-chugging of a locomotive echoed their way.

They were still a couple of miles out when weapons began barking—*pow-pow-pow!* Closing in at a canter and unsheathing their rifles, Lane and MacIver came to a grass-centered road trailing through trees and took it as their probing eyes picked out the gunrunners reeling away from the sustained rifle fire coming from the train that was stopped by a water tower, soldiers pouring out of the passenger cars coming after them. Some of the hardcases managed to reach their horses, but took to cover when cavalrymen began swooping in from the west.

Lane barked, "This means somebody in the army can read." He shaped a wicked grin for MacIver as a couple of horsemen bolted toward them, and separating, they took the hardcases out with a shot apiece.

"You're not bad," commented MacIver.

"Hope those soldiers don't take us for outlaws." Lane pumped the lever on his rifle as two riders broke out of an alley to jump their horses over a picket fence. A snap shot from Lane's long gun tore an outlaw out of the saddle. Spurring around, Lane cut out after the gunrunner clearing the outer limits of Big Timber.

After a while out on a vast sheet of tawny plain Lane realized he was gaining on the gunrunner, even though his own horse was tiring. "C'mon," he urged the canelo, "don't quit on me now."

Without warning, the gunrunner brought his galloping horse around and headed straight for Lane Jericho. Gripping the reins in his teeth, Jay Paragon unleathered both of his .45's and cut loose at Lane sweeping out his Smith & Wesson. When Lane's gun bucked, Paragon slumped in the saddle. Another slug striking the gunrunner made him sprawl over the shoulders of his horse and trigger his weapons harmlessly at the ground. A slug must have struck his horse, for it suddenly broke stride and reared, throwing Paragon out of the saddle. He hit hard, rolled over, and went limp.

As Lane slowed down the canelo, several horsemen swept over a hump of prairie. Closer, he determined one of them was his son, Brad, with morning sunlight glinting off the badge pinned to his shirt. Lane holstered his gun and folded his hands over the saddle horn. Suddenly he felt washed out, conscious of the throbbing pain coming from his shoulder, and just wanting to head out someplace again. Now the posse drew up around Lane and the dead gunrunner.

"That's Jay Paragon."

"Won't be bothering anybody again, Brad."

"Why didn't you tell me you're my pa?"

"Didn't want to invade your privacy. How'd you find out?"

"Your wife told me."

"Laurel?"

"Ma's back at White Sulphur Springs. She was witness to that gunfight back there."

Lane just sat there, his eyes going to the northern horizon.

"You didn't have to hit me so darned hard."

"Jerichos are thick-skulled people."

"Yeah, both of us are."

"What in tarnation is happening down there?" inquired Milo Thurmond.

"The U.S. Army is conducting summer exercises."

"That so? You two, throw that outlaw aboard his horse. Then we'll make tracks into town."

The Jerichos hung back as the posse headed out. Opening a can of snuff, Brad fingered some into his mouth and gummed it around, then he said, "What about you, where do you figure on heading?"

"Son," Lane said hesitantly, "probably to a peaceful spot far removed from Montana. Since I was told not too long ago to clear out of the territory. Should have stayed aboard that train. You?"

"Julia's back there. She'll need me now. Lane, I just want you to know that for some mysterious reason your wife still loves you. She was planning on going back to Bozeman, but didn't. You'll find her up there at the Regent Hotel. That is, if you feel the same way about her."

A sudden smile wiped away the sober set to Lane's face. "That would be something, me and your ma getting together again. Trouble is, Son—that is, if it's okay to call you that?"

"It don't hurt my ears none."

"Trouble is, I just wouldn't know what to say to her . . . to Laurel."

"You never had any trouble telling me how to act." Grinning, he added, "At least we'd be a family again . . . Pa." Reining closer to Lane, he held out his hand, and Lane grasped it along with giving his newfound son a hug.

"First we'll head back to Big Timber so's I can say my good-byes to that mountie, MacIver."

The shootout had roused the citizenry of Big Timber, and when the Jerichos passed through town, it was to find everyone clustered by the railroad tracks. Coming in at a walk, Lane squinted into the morning sun and glanced at Brad, "I'll be hornswoggled if that ain't Con Tillison."

"I thought you were Marshal Con Tillison—"

"The marshal loaned me his name . . . and troubles." He swung down and, with Brad at his

243

side, threaded through the crowd to pass alongside locomotive 553 and toward Tillison and MacIver clustered with several officers.

Right away Tillison spotted the Jerichos, and he said, "Colonel Travers, I want that ugly black-haired gent arrested for pretending to be a lawman."

"That so?"

"And if that isn't enough, he's a notorious gunslinger to boot."

Travers and everyone there broke out laughing, and when Lane came up, the colonel held out his hand and said, "Sergeant MacIver has filled us in on your fine work, Mr. Jericho."

"Shawn's a teller of tall tales." Dipping a hand into a vest pocket, Lane brought out Tillison's badge and handed it to the man. "Glad to be shed of that; mostly it's been an omen of bad luck. But there's one thing, Con. I figured the U.S. government owes me a heap of back pay for doing your job. So just tell me where to mail my pay voucher."

"You've got as much chance of collecting that, Lane, as I do of growing hair over my bald spot."

"Figures."

"But I can treat you to drinks and a meal or two."

"Being charity cases, my son and I'll take you up on that."

"So," said Shawn MacIver, "you did tell the lad."

"More or less. Mostly it was him."

The following morning the Jerichos caught the northern trail out of Big Timber. A doctor had tended to Lane's shoulder wound, while the comfort of a feather bed after several hours of being entertained by Tillison and the U.S. Army had taken away some of his aches. Still, he rode with a glint in his eyes, apprehensive over the upcoming encounter with Laurel. And to Brad's surprise, he'd stowed his Smith & Wesson in a saddlebag. Later that morning as they skirted the Crazies, Brad broke the long silence.

"I figure you're through packing a gun. Well, so am I."

"Meaning you're done marshaling?"

"I am," the younger Jericho said firmly. "Just might become a horse rancher."

"Son, I know two women who'll sure take to that notion."

EPILOGUE

Unlike most of those alighting from hansom cabs and carriages, the woman wearing a black dress and matching veiled hat carried no hand luggage as she hurried toward the gangplank. Her eyes flicked up at the transatlantic liner *Servia* registered out of Liverpool and powered by steam and sails. She knew that in about an hour the *Servia* would cast off her lines and be towed out into the Hudson and then embark for England. But of greater importance to Hannah Colmar was that the man she'd come to kill was aboard the *Servia*.

Hannah had left Fort Shaw a disgraced woman. But she'd blamed the death of her husband on Major Dirk Mackley, and could not believe Mackley had drowned in the Yellowstone River. So just before leaving the army post she'd stolen over to Mackley's quarters. Flin had sometimes told of the major leaving to go over to Billings to tend to business matters. That night she found what she needed in the bottom of a chest, a small leather-bound book which had in it entries penned in some kind

247

of code.

Upon arriving in Billings, Hannah checked into one of the best hotels. She spend the first few days in her room trying to make sense of the coded entries, each entry composed of a date with other figures, which could mean a sum of money, and the initials, A.C. Other cities were listed also. But to her the fact money was involved meant a banking institution.

Fortunately for Hannah, the city of Billings had only two banks, while she had determined that the initials A.C. could only mean an alias that Mackley had assumed. It was at the Cattleman's Bank that she struck up an acquaintance with a young teller while inquiring as to the best way to open a savings account. That conversation led to a dinner invitation. And so under the spell of Hannah's dark beauty the teller was only too glad to give her a name to the man she'd just described.

"Of course, Hannah, that could only be Arthur Covington."

"I was told that he had passed away."

"That must have been after he closed out his account with us."

"When was that?"

"Three weeks ago."

From Billings the trail took Hannah Colmar to other cities mentioned in Dirk Mackley's code book. In every instance accounts in other banks had been closed. And there was no trace of Dirk Mackley. Now her only recourse was to hire a private detective, who soon found out that a man matching Mackley's description had caught an eastbound train out of Denver. To New York, the detective had added.

The rest was merely anticlimatic for Hannah Colmar, the long train ride, further inquiries in that Eastern city about an Arthur Covington which ended up at the Biltmore Hotel and with the news that the man she was after had departed that very afternoon for Europe.

On board ship, Hannah slipped along the gleaming teak deck and then made her way down to the first-class staterooms. The passageway she moved along resounded with the excited voices of its new passengers and those who'd come to see them off. Except for a few men giving her admiring glances, she was just another member of this cosmopolitan crowd sailing for Europe. She'd learned that Mackley wasn't alone, for a young lady would be sharing his stateroom, and now there it was, number 1204. She slipped over to the open door to hear the murmur of voices coming from the adjoining bedroom. Easing into the small living room, Hannah closed the heavy steel door. From her purse she withdrew a Pepper-box revolver, her high-buttoned shoes making no sound on the plush carpeting. At the sound of Mackley's voice, she paused and choked down the fear causing her to tremble.

"You'll be the toast of London, my dear."

"Arthur, I'm so excited. And this champagne tickles my nose."

In the living room the bitter memories of what this man had done to her gave Hannah the courage she needed to go on with this. Firming her grip on the revolver, she stepped toward the open doorway.

249

At first the woman took Hannah to be another passenger or a friend of Mackley's, but the welcome smile froze when she saw the gun. As she cowed back against the bed, Dirk Mackley spun around spilling champagne on the floor.

"What the—" he bared his teeth when he saw the gun. "I never expected to be robbed on a transatlantic liner."

"This isn't a robbery, Mr. Covington."

"Do I . . . know you?"

All Hannah could see at that moment was Dirk Mackley tearing at her clothing before he had his way with her. Somehow she controlled her terrible anger as she hissed, "You murdered my husband, Mr. Mackley . . . took your pleasure with me!"

"Hannah?" He began edging toward her, still not believing that she meant him any harm.

"Yes . . . Hannah." Lifting her veil, Hannah placed her other hand on the gun and pulled the trigger, kept pulling it as Mackley staggered. Only two slugs missed the man she hated, but those scoring into his body sent the renegade army officer falling onto the woman who'd just passed out on the bed. Then out of sightless eyes he gazed up at Hannah Colmar.

Calmly, and without any remorse, Hannah let the revolver fall from her trembling hands. She hurried out of the stateroom as the *Servia*'s whistle sounded to tell everyone it was sailing time. Down on the pier, Hannah clambered into a hansom cab and told the driver to drop her off at the Metropole.

As the cab rolled away, a boy hawking newspapers yelled out, "Extra! Extra! Read all about it in the *Chronicle!* Rebellion put down in Canada! Extra!"

The words had little meaning to Hannah or to those lining the rails aboard the *Servia* as the great ship slipped away from its moorings. For her thoughts had slipped back to Fort Shaw in Montana Territory and to all that had happened. And around a pensive smile she murmured, "It's over, Flin . . . so adieu, my darling . . ."

POWELL'S ARMY
BY TERENCE DUNCAN

#1: UNCHAINED LIGHTNING   (1994, $2.50)
Thundering out of the past, a trio of deadly enforcers dispenses its own brand of frontier justice throughout the untamed American West! Two men and one woman, they are the U.S. Army's most lethal secret weapon—they are POWELL'S ARMY!

#2: APACHE RAIDERS   (2073, $2.50)
The disappearance of seventeen Apache maidens brings tribal unrest to the violent breaking point. To prevent an explosion of bloodshed, Powell's Army races through a nightmare world south of the border—and into the deadly clutches of a vicious band of Mexican flesh merchants!

#3: MUSTANG WARRIORS   (2171, $2.50)
Someone is selling cavalry guns and horses to the Comanche—and that spells trouble for the bluecoats' campaign against Chief Quanah Parker's bloodthirsty Kwahadi warriors. But Powell's Army are no strangers to trouble. When the showdown comes, they'll be ready—and someone is going to die!

#4: ROBBERS ROOST   (2285, $2.50)
After hijacking an army payroll wagon and killing the troopers riding guard, Three-Fingered Jack and his gang high-tail it into Virginia City to spend their ill-gotten gains. But Powell's Army plans to apprehend the murderous hardcases before the local vigilantes do—to make sure that Jack and his slimy band stretch hemp the legal way!

ACTION ADVENTURE

SILENT WARRIORS (1675, $3.95)
by Richard P. Henrick

The Red Star, Russia's newest, most technologically advanced submarine, outclasses anything in the U.S. fleet. But when the captain opens his sealed orders 24 hours early, he's staggered to read that he's to spearhead a massive nuclear first strike against the Americans!

THE PHOENIX ODYSSEY (1789, $3.95)
by Richard P. Henrick

All communications to the USS *Phoenix* suddenly and mysteriously vanish. Even the urgent message from the president cancelling the War Alert is not received. In six short hours the *Phoenix* will unleash its nuclear arsenal against the Russian mainland.

COUNTERFORCE (2013, $3.95)
Richard P. Henrick

In the silent deep, the chase is on to save a world from destruction. A single Russian Sub moves on a silent and sinister course for American shores. The men aboard the U.S.S. *Triton* must search for and destroy the Soviet killer Sub as an unsuspecting world races for the apocalypse.

EAGLE DOWN (1644, $3.75)
by William Mason

To western eyes, the Russian Bear appears to be in hibernation — but half a world away, a plot is unfolding that will unleash its awesome, deadly power. When the Russian Bear rises up, God help the Eagle.

DAGGER (1399, $3.50)
by William Mason

The President needs his help, but the CIA wants him dead. And for Dagger — war hero, survival expert, ladies man and mercenary extraordinaire — it will be a game played for keeps.

ASHES
by William W. Johnstone

OUT OF THE ASHES   (1137, $3.50)

Ben Raines hadn't looked forward to the War, but he knew it was coming. After the balloons went up, Ben was one of the survivors, fighting his way across the country, searching for his family, and leading a band of new pioneers attempting to bring American OUT OF THE ASHES.

FIRE IN THE ASHES   (1310, $3.50)

It's 1999 and the world as we know it no longer exists. Ben Raines, leader of the Resistance, must regroup his rebels and prep them for bloody guerrilla war. But are they ready to face an even fiercer foe—the human mutants threatening to overpower the world!

ANARCHY IN THE ASHES   (2592, $3.95)

Out of the smoldering nuclear wreckage of World War III, Ben Raines has emerged as the strong leader the Resistance needs. When Sam Hartline, the mercenary, joins forces with an invading army of Russians, Ben and his people raise a bloody banner of defiance to defend earth's last bastion of freedom.

SMOKE FROM THE ASHES   (2191, $3.50)

Swarming across America's Southern tier march the avenging soldiers of Libyan blood terrorist Khamsin. Lurking in the blackened ruins of once-great cities are the mutant Night People, crazed killers of all who dare enter their domain. Only Ben Raines, his son Buddy, and a handful of Ben's Rebel Army remain to strike a blow for the survival of America and the future of the free world!

ALONE IN THE ASHES   (2591, $3.95)

In this hellish new world there are human animals and Ben Raines—famed soldier and survival expert—soon becomes their hunted prey. He desperately tries to stay one step ahead of death, but no one can survive ALONE IN THE ASHES.

Available wherever paperbacks are sold, or order direct from the Publisher. Send cover price plus 50¢ per copy for mailing and handling to Zebra Books, Dept. 2509, 475 Park Avenue South, New York, N.Y. 10016. Residents of New York, New Jersey and Pennsylvania must include sales tax. DO NOT SEND CASH.